HIS FIRST, BEST COUNTRY

HIS FIRST,
BEST COUNTRY

Jim Wayne Miller

GNOMON PRESS

FIRST EDITION

This project is supported by grants from the
National Endowment for the Arts, A Federal
Agency, and the Kentucky Arts Council.

Copyright (c) 1993 by Jim Wayne Miller

ISBN 0-917788-54-0 (cloth)
ISBN 0-917788-55-9 (paper)
LCCC 92-75360

Published by GNOMON PRESS,
P.O. Box 475, Frankfort,
Kentucky 40602-0475

1

Dear Gerald,

Remember that night back on Doggett Mountain when you drove to our camp at Double Springs, bouncing over the dark fields in a log truck, dodging dead chestnuts, bringing two half-gallons of white whiskey from Bud Reams'?

I remember you said you were going to Detroit. Remember I said I'd write you. And that's all I remember.

They said I got in Ted Scott's Mercury—and passed out on the horn. And since I'd locked myself inside—why, I don't know—and couldn't be roused, you all left—your crowd and mine, and spent the rest of the night out of hearing of that horn.

I guess they told the truth, for when I woke next morning, the battery in the Mercury was dead, and I was hung way over. And you were gone and I've not seen you since. That was twenty-seven, twenty-eight years ago.

I said I'd write, though, so I'm writing.

I don't think you've been home since 1966. So it's not likely you know how Newfound's changed (not likely, either, you give a damn). But I'm going to tell you, anyway.

This place where we grew up, rough as a cob, dumb as a coal bucket, it's on the map now. God knows, we didn't put it there, and wouldn't have if we'd stayed on. But where we filled your Daddy's silos, and housed burley tobacco by the acre, and then drove trucks and jeeps up creek beds till daylight (I wonder if we ever slept at all)—this place. . . .

By the way, your Daddy died. Did anybody write or call? (My Dad died five years ago, and Mama this past winter.)

Remember that farm your Daddy wanted you to take over, the one your brother-in-law wouldn't touch, either? Your Daddy even tried to strike a deal with me. Well, your Mama, over the years, has sold it off in tracts and parcels.

A retired inventor of something, from New York, bought everything on the Little Sandy side.

Some kind of cult or commune of Jesus people bought the old homeplace. Local people call them Hare Krishnas, but they're not. I'm told that Arlis Surrett was breaking newground up there after the Jesus people moved in. Arlis looked between his mule's ears toward the line fence, saw somebody in a white robe walking down the ridge—and left plow and mule standing in the newground, thought for the longest time he'd seen Jesus.

We've got the Jesus people here in the eastern end of Cordell County, and a pack of back-to-the-landers growing organic crops, Nubian goats, living in renovated barns, mobile homes and geodesic domes. The other end of the county, where the coal seams run, is pretty well trashed, or scheduled to be trashed by strip mining.

The back-to-the-landers have put out this book—I bought it for three dollars—called the *Southern Appalachian Resource Catalogue*. Newfound's there—our place—on a map that's a center fold out in the book. We're number 36. The number identifies "Sandy Mush Creek Herbs on the Surrett Cove Road. Herb growers; visits by appointment." And next to that, "The Nothing But Natural Food Store" on Elk Street in Jewell Hill. You wouldn't believe the crowd that's moved in: spinners, dyers, weavers. They're big on doing stuff Grandma Wells only half-remembered. Up on Sugar Creek they teach midwifery. Somebody makes candles and raises Angora goats—"the mohair fleece is excellent for handspinning."

They advertise their wares and services in the catalog. Somebody's selling Inner G bars and Loveburgers, "natural alternatives," it says, "to meat and sugar." There's a Babyland General Hospital that has "little people soft sculpture babies—up for adoption."

Want to learn white water rafting? There's a writer/poet/ runner, haiku-maker and publisher of poetry, fiction, and energy, who'll teach you.

(Maybe I don't have any room to talk. For as your Aunt Vashti once put it, I went off to school and "made a teacher." Wrote some books. May write a few more.)

But about the catalog: there's this couple, Bob and Barbara. He's a professional T'ai Chi instructor; she's an astrologer who does soul portraits and charts your rhythms and cycles.

The woods are full of solar carpenters, potters, spiritualists, dulcimer makers, calligraphers, rice cake makers, "human resource development consultants." There's a specialist in appropriate technology, a hang-gliding instructor. We used to have the Rocky Top Festival, right here in Cordell County, and did our own singing, square and circle dancing, clogging. Now we have the services of somebody, advertised in this catalog, as a dance caller for New England contras.

Used to be you went up Surrett Cove to buy white liquor or

3

get your ashes hauled—or both. Somebody up there now practices "holistic medicine" out of a doublewide. Somebody else, according to an ad in the catalog, is an "artisan in fudge."

Did you have some kind of early warning system, Gerald? Did you foresee all this? Is that why you got out so fast and never came back? I left so gradually—going to school, then teaching, but always coming and going between Newfound and school—I was a long time realizing what was happening—to me, and to this place.

It's strange who left, stranger who stayed. My little brother Eugene runs a big filling station in California. My sister Jeanette married into the military. She and her husband have lived everywhere. Right now they're at a base in Alabama. Roseanne Shelton left. Lord, I loved that girl. For a long time I couldn't understand how she and Hilliard could be brother and sister. Finally, I saw they were actually just alike—and that cured me.

Surely you remember Hilliard Shelton. Hilliard stayed on, and according to his lights he's done right well. Big fine house with columns—looks like a courthouse. I take that back—more like a funeral home. House is so big Hilliard and Hilda have intercoms in the house to talk to one another. Had Hilliard already married Hilda Goad before you left? Hilliard and Hilda. Hilliard flies a big flag out front. Gazebo down by the road. Hilliard stayed on, Roseanne left. I would have thought it would be the other way around. I guess because I wished it that way. They say Hilliard drives Hilda into Jewell Hill every day for breakfast. And takes her to New York or Dallas or Los Angeles twice a year to shop and get some culture.

Anyway, after all the years, I've come back home with the thought of staying awhile, maybe for good. But as I pulled in

4

tonight and saw the old place in the headlights, the thought struck me: I don't live here any longer.

And yet, let a drizzly Sunday morning in the fall come and I always want to drink white liquor and play poker in a gray barn where burley's hanging cured.

But it's hard to find a plain old barn here in Newfound now. Most of the barns and old houses have been turned into places "where kindred cosmic souls come together" (that's from the catalog). You can't play poker and drink white where that sort of thing is going on.

Tell you what I've done though: I bought the old Shelton house—from the Army Corps of Engineers. The one old Hilliard grew up in, and Roseanne, too. I'm going to have it taken down and put back together here at home.

I missed getting a chance to bid on the Shelton barn and crib, and smokehouse. They went to a museum over in Tennessee.

Do you know of any old barns, a smokehouse, maybe, where we could drive trucks and jeeps, and get together on a Sunday morning?

This is the letter I said I'd write you—all those years ago.

If I knew where you were, I'd mail it to you.

Your cousin,
Robert Jennings Wells

Heading home last night, driving into a storm, he'd turned his headlights on and watched limbs of lightning play over the mountains up ahead. Slipping along on the interstate in his Skyhawk, moving through east Tennessee on a Sunday at the edge of dark in late August, Jennings Wells had felt uneasy. He should be feeling good, he'd told himself. He was going

5

home, the Skyhawk stuffed with clothes, books, papers, his typewriter. Home. For four months. Maybe longer, depending on how things went. But at least for four months he wouldn't be plagued by classes, seminars, appointments and deadlines. He could work at his own pace. On what *he* wanted to write. Not what some editor wanted. Or he could do nothing, if that suited him.

For too long now his brain, that pale, dry-palmed professor, had written so many little essays, prefaces, introductions to other people's work, he'd come to think of himself as a humming bird, a flash of brilliance hovering over this geranium, that morning glory, or a swallow building nests in abandoned barns. Meanwhile his own work waited, like a stable of horses left pawing in their stalls. So he'd taken a leave from flitting flower to flower; from gathering string and horsehair; from hunching like a soft-handed clerk chained to his desk. He was coming home, to turn his own little horses out their black barn door, and let them go galloping across green fields.

Still he felt uneasy. Those were not green fields falling away on either side of the highway, but brown, dry, end-of-summer fields dotted with cedars. His Skyhawk droned on at a legal 65, past a state policeman crouched in his cruiser behind an abutment at an overpass. Lightning flickered more ominously up ahead. And as he scanned stations, the radio reminded him that the mountains were never as he remembered them when he was away from them. The avalanche of junk that tumbled from the radio, like trash swept down a flooding creek, depressed him: country music; ads for meat tenderizer and toothpaste; country music; more ads for cat and dog food and treatment against roundworms, just before a warning to illegal aliens, followed by hype for mobile homes, then gospel music sponsored by headache powders, followed by stock car races brought to

6

the folks in Radio Land by Black Draught (this was as it should be). Country music. A get-right-with-God evangelist who read a letter from a listener (and generous contributor to his ministry) who'd had an ugly growth removed from a private place by faith alone. A money-grubbing motive sat in every pitch, like the billboard in that clump of trees. Like the Chew Mail Pouch sign on the old barn (he could hardly see it now as night came on). Big trucks came grunting up behind him and swung out and moved past like cruising fish, leaving him in a heaving wake of air. He felt uneasy.

Maybe it had been the storm he'd headed into. Tires whining, he rolled over the bridge across the Holston River towards Newfound and remembered the time (from here on to Newfound the land held memories for him) when he and his father and his Uncle Roy had rescued a thirsty fisherman there one evening years ago after the fisherman had been abandoned on the bank by his drunken buddies. That reminded him of the old man who backed over his Coleman camp stove in the fog early on Labor Day at Lake Santeetlah—when? It must have been 1952. The old man's truck had smashed the stove, but it had been dumb of Jennings to set the stove up in that flat place where the old man came in the foggy dawn to turn his truck. Jennings had taken five dollars from the old man and spoiled the old man's day at the lake (the man, he later learned, had been saving that five dollars to rent a boat). Jennings remembered how he'd seen the old man fishing from the bank, and how, ever since, whenever he saw a stump, a rock, a piece of gray driftwood by a lakeshore, he thought of that old man, in a bleached denim jumper, fishing from the bank. That old man who, after thirty years, must be dead by now. Like Jennings' father. Like his Uncle Roy.

As he started up into the mountains, he'd hit a sudden wall

7

of rain. He set the wipers to working frantically. Wind buffeted the Skyhawk. He drove on slowly but soon pulled off onto the shoulder and sat with his blinkers flashing, waiting for the rain to slack off. Sat remembering another mountain road and the time, when he was sixteen and in love with speed, he'd run over Jess Teague's turkey, and how his father had paid Jess fifteen dollars for the old tom.

When the rain let up, he'd driven on. By the time he left the interstate for the winding state road, he wondered if Newfound held anything but memories for him. Was it a place he could really come back to? Except to visit? All the years he'd been away from it, he'd loved this place. But through all those years, whenever he'd come home, the closer he got the more he was reminded of why he'd left in the first place.

He passed The Trading Post at the forks of the creek and headed up the Early's Gap Road. He had driven out of the storm. The night was still again. His headlights picked up the old white mailbox. He turned off the road and headed up the drive. His headlights raked the big barn, the silo; then, as he turned toward the house, his headlights suddenly burned like candles in the windowpanes of the dark house.

He got out of the car and stood a minute, listening to the maples dripping rain. So familiar, yet so strange. And silent except for the dripping trees. He stood a long time holding the house key in his hand. When finally he climbed the porch steps, turned the key in the lock and stepped inside, he paused again, smelling the mustiness of the closed house. He hadn't been there since April, and then only for a weekend.

Some homecoming this was.

He felt for the switch in the dark, turned on a light, and looked around at the familiar surroundings. His father's old recliner, his mother's rocker by the pole lamp. Out in the kitchen, magazines he'd left on the table when he'd worked there back in April. A wastebasket full of old notes and draft pages. That piece he'd written still hadn't appeared, and the editor had been in such a rush for it.

He brought a few things in from the Skyhawk—coffee, he'd remembered to bring coffee—put on a pot, and sat looking through the magazines he'd left there. Came on *The Southern Appalachian Resource Catalog,* something he'd picked up somewhere and remembered looking through ruefully back in the spring. Leafing through the magazine again (it was hardly a catalog), he thought of his cousin Gerald, who'd also left Newfound many years ago. He'd dreamed about Gerald two or three times lately. Maybe that dream had to do with his uneasiness about coming back to Newfound.

After the six-hour drive, he should have been tired. Instead, his thoughts flitting like night birds, he'd felt peculiarly alert, even before the coffee was ready. And after drinking two cups and flipping back through *The Southern Appalachian Resource Catalog,* sleep was out of the question. He kept thinking about his cousin Gerald, wondering where he was, what Gerald had been doing all these years. He pulled a sheaf of old notes out of the wastebasket and started scribbling a letter to Gerald, using the backs of the pages.

He'd tinkered with the letter, flipping back and forth in the catalog for items, for a couple of hours before he'd finally slept. On the sofa. In the living room.

Now, after making a fresh pot of coffee, he sat reading over what he'd written in the night. Reading and thinking. Before he came home this time, he'd been full of certainties. Now that he was here, he realized he wasn't sure of anything. He hadn't

9

meant to write a mock letter to his cousin, but there it was, scrawled across the backs of several pages of old notes.

He sat there a long time thinking about how he was forever being surprised by what he thought, or felt, or meant, for he never knew exactly until he'd said it.

2

That first day back in Newfound, for the first time in years, Jennings Wells walked about the old homeplace. Two hundred and fifty acres, barns, silos, and in addition to the two-story white house his Grandfather and Grandmother Wells had lived in, the old gray sharecropper house up the holler. There he'd lived with his mother and brother and sister, Eugene and Jeanette, after his mother and father had separated and his mother came back to live with her parents on a farm owned by her husband's parents! He remembered when it had dawned on him, at about the age of ten, what an odd situation theirs was. Two other sharecropper houses across the ridge.

He crossed the barbed wire fence and walked far down the point, until he could see an arm of the lake—the old Newfound Creek bed—lying blue and still in the sun. He remembered more than he saw—remembered the old man, one of the Sutherlands, who bottomed chairs, and who'd come through every spring, lean and long-legged, with a huge bundle of green oak splints balanced on his back. In Jennings' memory the old man came walking now, like a water sprinter over the still surface of—how many summers? On the green lawn, between the porch and the foot log over the branch, there at his Grandfather and Grandmother Smith's, the old man would strip their chairs of old and broken splints and weave new bottoms with the green one from his pack, or else with sea grass string. Those chairs, scattered in half a dozen attics now, in barn lofts, upside down and broken, lost in hay. Jennings made a green place in the shade of remembering the old chair bottomer and in his mind the scattered chairs righted themselves as old ghosts grew warm, and, rocking, whispered tales to each other by open fires.

But that was revery. What he saw was broomsage, cedars, sumac, second growth. . . .

And the good grey barn closest to the creek, that had blown down in a windstorm. It lay now like the wreck of some great bird—rows of broken rafters under rusted tin like the fractured bones of wings stretched on rosy broomsage. From the crushed rib cage of tier poles, splintered ends jutted through weathered silvery boards that feathered out over flattened straw. He remembered how, when he was a boy, an owl would hoot from the barn on frost-bound nights. And he'd pretend it was the barn that hooted. Now he knew he'd miss the barn, old friend. It had always seemed to sit patient by Newfound Creek, like a kingfisher looking down into the water. . . .

Did everything have to come crashing down leaving him with nothing but recollection? Maybe he'd salvage the boards, the beams, the tier poles.

Everybody who ever lived here had left something, he thought. Indians camped by Newfound Creek left arrowheads. He used to find them every spring, when bottom land along the creek was plowed. Britts, Devashers, Penningtons (his Grand-father Wells' sharecroppers) left little family cemeteries—and a ditch of rusted car bodies and coffee cans. Now here I come, Jennings thought, with an uneasy suspicion that this place was finally claiming him, after all the years of absence. What would he leave, if he decided to stay? His poems, the way the Indians left chipped flint? The way settlers in Newfound left hand-hewn tombstones, gray goodbyes? Already, coming home wasn't feeling like he'd imagined it would be.

He'd imagined it would be exhilarating—coming home, on leave from the university, with the possibility that the home-coming would be permanent. Instead, he was discovering that moving the spirit to another place was dreary business. He could imagine old rocking chairs by a cozy fire. But only for a moment. Now his mind seemed a clean swept floor, an un-furnished room empty of all but someone else's smell, with no chair to be at ease in. He felt as if he had gone on ahead of himself, and parts of him were still arriving, like lost luggage sent on a piece at a time.

Dammit, he wanted this to work out! Wanted time—empty mornings, appointment-free afternoons—to finish a book that had been hanging fire. Wanted to get to know this place again, maybe discover a new vein of poems.

He stood looking across the arm of the lake to the cutover ridge. Saplings dwarfed second growth like lean schoolteachers in a thicket of third graders. Coming back up from the point, he walked the wagon road past the middle barn. With a few sticks of burley tobacco hanging in a side room, the barn put Jennings in mind of an old man with a good chew in his jaw. Why was everything reminding him of people?

Back at the house, from sheer habit, he tried to make notes. But his pencil point circled over the paper, like a hawk hovering, like a dog that turns around three times following his tail before lying down.

Restless, uncertain, he got into his car and drove around. Yesterday he'd flown from Washington back to the university, packed a few things, and driven straight to Newfound. Now here he was, out in the country, back home. On a day in late August after a night storm. On the seat beside him he had a xerox copy of a diary kept by a teacher of the Brick Church subscription school here at the foot of Hanlon Mountain. At a stop sign Jennings flipped through it to find: "Thurs. Sept. 3, 1896. Cloudy. Attended church."

He thought of the passing years, the changing seasons. His view of Newfound was a split image: what he remembered, what he saw now. When he was growing up here, these woods and fields had been full of gnomes. Trolls came out from under the bridge and walked along Temporary 63. At least, he'd once imagined it was so. But he knew now that had only been wart-faced Clayton Rogers, who took short cuts through the woods, a huge bundle of laundry balanced on his back like a beatle with an outsized ball of dung, humping home to his wife, her slat bonnet, her steaming black wash pot out by the smokehouse.

Or it had only been Whitey King, the red-eyed albino, or Running Jack Sterling, trotting away from the County Home, or Weaver Sams, there on Hanlon Mountain, whose cabin Jennings had come down to once in September. No, it must have been October, because he'd found Weaver sitting in the open door, listening to the World Series on a battery-powered radio, eating chinquapins, blowing the black hulls off his tongue into the dirt yard. A retired car dealer from Florida had a house on Hanlon now.

Chinquapins. They always reminded him of Roseanne Shelton. Her bright black eyes . . . like chinquapins. He wondered

14

where she was now, all these years later. The last he'd heard, that was years ago, she was somewhere in Ohio, still singing, and she'd had a kid she'd brought back to Newfound and left with her parents, who were still living in the old log house on the upper end of the lake. But wouldn't be living there long. Maybe, after he moved the log house up here, he could rebuild the blown-down barn close to it.

Or maybe not. Why did he feel so tentative, driving around in this thoroughly familiar place? This was his home. Why did he feel like such an interloper? He'd written about this place, described the pleasures of an old-fashioned way of life, the knowledge and serenity that came of living a long time in one place. Maybe he'd written about it so much, and spoken about it in so many places—maybe that was why he'd come to feel harried and distracted.

In 1907, he noticed, flipping through pages of the diary on the seat beside him, the teacher of the subscription school here had written: "Am hearty but nervous." Remembering the meeting in Washington last week (he was a board member of an educational service providing television programming for the Appalachian region), he thought he knew how the teacher back in 1907 had felt. He'd sat puzzling over a budget whose figures were expressed in thousands. The chairman had said: "A motion has been made. . . ." An executive director said: "Move on to the next slide." The board member beside him said: "You indicate there are forty-five stations receiving our programs, but what is the universe?"

During the past few days he had smelled honeysuckle and gunpowder, jet fuel and hot cornbread. He'd heard punk rock and foxhounds, felt crushed velvet and a mule's nose. He'd passed through a smokehouse door and airport metal detectors. In his Grandmother and Grandfather Wells' house, flipping

15

through an album, he'd come on the picture of a pretty girl his father had once pointed to and said: "That one like to have been your Mama."

Scattered thoughts and recollections. Am hearty but nervous, he thought. But what is the universe? he asked himself, remembering the board meeting in Washington.

Maybe he shouldn't be so impatient. It would take time to make this move in his mind. He'd give himself a few days to settle in, then get down to work.

He drove back to the old two-story white house, sat on the porch looking down the drive to the mailbox where he used to catch the school bus. In dry late-August grass by the porch corner, one cricket chirped feebly, like a fiddler with cold fingers. He wondered if he were caught up in some self-deception. How long would it be before he could feel he was back home?

3

Standing on the bridge over Newfound Creek, looking down into the dark water slipping under the bridge, Jennings realized he'd stopped the car and walked onto the bridge out of old habit. There'd been an old bridge here years ago, a wooden bridge, and it was to that bridge they'd come in late winter and early spring to watch for the arrival of redhorse, a fish that ran up the creeks like salmon. He stared into the pool below, occasionally shaking his head, remembering those days, and the men and boys he ran with.

He'd lived for woods and waters in those days, he and his buddies, passionate hunters and fishermen. He recalled now how their rifles had cracked on the ridges and in the hollows, how they would come off the slopes knee-deep and noisy in red and yellow leaves, guns in the crook of their arms, the tails of gray squirrels flying from every pocket. He could remember now the feel of a still-warm squirrel's body against his thigh, limp as after love. He recollected how they'd come home from a hunt, just before daylight, riding the fenders of a jeep or pickup full of hounds, their rifle butts resting on their thighs, ready for the fox or possum or coon whose eyes glowed in the head-lights. It seemed to him now they'd been bloodthirsty mountain boys. For even the pockets of their hunting clothes drank up the cooling blood of squirrels and rabbits, pheasants and partridges stuffed into them. Instead of money, they'd carried dried blood in their pockets.

But it seemed to him now, remembering, that what they'd really thirsted for was not blood but miracles. For when the rabbit bounded out of a clump of broomsage, or when the squir-rel sat in his sights, tail jerking, or when the pheasant roared up at his feet and flew, twisting and turning through the tim-ber, it was the awe that sowed itself like melting frost along his bones, and bloomed, ice crystals in his stomach—it was that awe that drew him into the woods again and again.

The woods had been a faith they lived by, every bird or ani-mal that swung into their sights a revelation. Killing them was just their clumsy, ignorant way of trying to hold a wonder in their hands. The miracle that was a squirrel or pheasant, its perfect, sleek wildness, had never failed to amaze him, awe him into a more perfect worship of the woods.

Unable to say it, still he'd known that certain things were beautiful. And he guessed the men and boys he hunted with felt the same way. They'd mistaken the shine of a steel trap, the aura of the clean kill, the brilliant fish leaping on a line, moonlight on a blue gun barrel, the eyes of a coon, caught in a flashlight's beam, glowing like banked fire—they mistook that light for the shine around the lives of animals, the brilliance of their strength and speed and suppleness. All the time they'd been trying to hold fire in their hands; they'd been trying to reach out, wanting to touch, to draw a wonder close and hold it still, the better to be amazed.

That was why—for they hadn't really been bloodthirsty—that was why they'd let their hands grow guns, steel traps, and hooks. He thought he understood now that back then they'd been like children making shadows on a wall: they'd held their hands before the light of their lives, and shaped them into shadowheads of hounds, and loosed them, frothy-mouthed, into the woods.

But every time they'd tried to hold in their hands the wonder that was the life of something wild, they'd had to watch the wonder fade, grow dim and lusterless, breathed out in bloody bubbles through the nose. They had to feel the last heartbeats flutter inside the soft rib cage; they had to see the brilliant fish, speckled, streaked, barred, go pale on their stringer. Birds and animals brought in the jaws of hounds fell at their feet, wet and rumpled, like bedraggled stuffed toys. The eyes of partridges and pheasants clouded over; the shine of their life, like sunlight leaving a field of broomsage, like fur that glistened and shone when muscles rippled underneath, left forever.

They'd been lethal believers, living to be amazed. Still, their death-dealing touch had given glimpses, even as the shine faded from the life of some bird or fish or animal. Glimpses. Maybe that was why they'd killed again and again. They'd killed for imperfect fleeting glimpses, for the opportunity to come so close to something amazing and beautiful.

Now he felt tired, and so far from that country he remembered when the redhorse ran up the creeks in spring. Could he go there again simply by coming home?

4

That afternoon, his first Monday back home, he drove down to
The Trading Post to see if he could round up a few men to dismantle the old Shelton house. Delano Crumm, Dee Rhodommer, and Wiley Woolford hung out regularly at The Trading
Post, Jennings knew, and if they couldn't be hired, they would
know who could be.

Sure enough, half a dozen men and boys—Delano, Dee,
and Wiley among them—occupied the loafers bench out by
the horseshoe pits. Their presence was reassuring to Jennings:
some things never changed. He observed the etiquette of talking
about everything else before getting around to the real purpose
of his visit.

When did Jennings get home? they wanted to know.

Was he still teaching over at that college?

How long was he back home for?

Wiley Woolford remembered something Jennings' father had
said at The Trading Post one time. Somebody had asked old

man Chris Wells, "Have you read Jennings' last book?"—and Jennings' Dad had said, "I hope so."

Jennings grinned. "Turned out, he hadn't."

"Thought the world of old man Chris Wells," Dee Rhodommer said.

Delano Crumm regretted his mother's death back in the winter.

Some weather we were having, so hot and dry. That little rain last night hadn't hardly settled the dust.

Word had already reached the loafers at The Trading Post that he'd bought the Shelton house. And, yeah, Delano Crumm might be able to dismantle it for Jennings, haul it over to his house there, if that's where he wanted it. Though it was hard for Delano to understand what anybody wanted with these old log houses. He was born and brought up in one, and it wasn't any fun when cold wind whipped through the cracks in the walls and you woke up a winter morning with a dusting of snow on your blanket.

Dee Rhodommer remembered going out barefoot to drive cows to the milk gap on frosty fall mornings, and his feet would be so cold he'd stand on the ground where the cows had lain all night just to warm his feet.

What did Jennings want with that old Shelton house, anyway?

Jennings cocked his head, squatting there beside the loafers bench. He hardly knew what to say. It was a nice old house, one of the oldest in the county. He guessed he just wanted to keep it in the county, where it belonged. So many had been bought and hauled off some place else.

Jennings was sure right about that.

And there'd been two or three movies made around New-found, and it seemed like the movie people always wanted to use old log houses in the movies. Was Jennings thinking about making a movie?

No, he just wanted to re-assemble the house there at home sometime. He cautioned that he wanted the logs marked so he could put the house back just as it had been.

Delano Crumm knew all about that. He had torn down two or three old houses for people who'd come through Newfound buying them up—old houses and barns. But Miz McCreary's smokehouse—that topped everything.

Jennings knew from Delano's tone that he was in for a story.

"Yeah?" he said. "Who bought Miz McCreary's smokehouse?"

"I did," Delano said. "At least, that's how it all started. I was up there at her place in my truck one day, hauling something for her, I believe. She said how much would I give her for them logs in her smokehouse. She didn't use the smokehouse anymore. I didn't need them but I knowed she wouldn't have offered to sell them if she hadn't wanted them off the place, or needed money. I said I'd give her ten dollars for them and haul them off."

Delano tipped his hat back and ran his fingers through his grey hair. "Well, that old smokehouse had mostly fell in on itself. When I went back up there to haul it off, I had to run Miz McCreary's cows away from it. They'd stand and lick the logs for the salt in them. You know, where meat had been salted down in that smokehouse.

"After I knocked the old smokehouse down and hauled it home," Delano said, "them logs lay stacked for, I guess, a year or more. Then I sold them—to a feller named Tweed. For $35.00. But Tweed never got around to hauling them off, so they stayed stacked there for another year. Yeah, at least a year. I saw Tweed over in Jewell Hill and he asked me would I buy them logs back from him. I did—for $25.00." Delano winked at Jennings.

22

"Then the TVA got interested in them logs. They aimed to build log cabins, put them on truck beds, make what they called a 'mobile museum'—haul them around to show folks how it was back in the old days. They eventually did put four or five of them mobile museums into operation, I heard tell. Spent close to a million dollars doing it, is what I heard. But I'm getting ahead of myself.

"See, at first the TVA wasn't interested in *old* logs. They'd hired a company out of New York to build a 'pilot' log cabin. The folks in New York subcontracted to a company in Chicago. Well, sir, a call come down out of Chicago: 'Christ, we've got problems here!' Problem was, they were having trouble in Chicago making new logs look like old logs, old weathered logs. And another thing, these artists they had on the job had problems joining the logs at the corners."

"You're kidding me, Delano," Jennings said.

"Hit's the tom-truth!" Wiley Woolford said.

Delano held up his hand, as if he were swearing an oath.

"It's so," Wiley Woolford nodded.

"So they flew somebody in over at Bristol, made field trips, looked at a lot of old log houses, took pictures, called all around. Flew back to Chicago, then back to Bristol, drove around out in here in a rented car. That's when they come to me, heard I had them logs from Miz McCreary's smokehouse. Wanted to know would I sell 'em. I did—for $800.00."

Jennings said, "Delano, you're just telling a tall one."

"Don't trade pocketknives with this jasper," Dee Rhodommer said, jerking his thumb at Delano. "Unless you want to get slicked."

"I've got the papers on it still, somewhere. The sales slip. Why, they sent two trucks in here, wrapped them logs every one in a separate shipping quilt, hauled them to Chicago. After that they hired me on to advise them on the project."

"Paid you for that, too, I guess," Jennings said.

"Paid right well. I give them an old iron kettle to go in the cabin they built. Didn't charge them for that. Just throwed that in, part of the deal. Then, I reckon it was three or four years after I sold them the logs, they had that cabin they made out of them on a flatbed truck over here on the school ground, showing it to the younguns—in full view of Miz McCreary's house, and the very spot where that old smokehouse had stood for maybe a hundred years."

"You did all right on that deal, didn't you, Delano?" Jennings said.

"I'd reckon."

"You're not gonna slick me the way you did those fellows from Chicago?"

"I'll treat you right," Delano said, and tipped his hat back again and scratched his head. "But that went on for several years. I went over there to the school and stepped up in that log cabin and looked around at what they'd done. It would have been a good week's work, maybe, for me and Dee and Wiley here. And I know we could have brought the job in for under $900,000, which is what I think they said it cost. Or maybe that was all four or five they made cost that much, I disremember."

"I was hoping I could get that house taken down and hauled over home and stacked up, till I can get time to think about putting it back together, for—I thought maybe—three or four hundred dollars." Jennings gauged Delano's reaction.

Delano's right eye squinted, his chin jutted out.

"I'm not the TVA," Jennings said.

"I believe I can do it for that," Delano said.

"All right."

"Come home, have you?"

24

"Maybe. Maybe. I'm going to be here for awhile, anyway."

"You know that kettle I give them fellers—that iron kettle?" Delano said. "When I stepped up in that house and looked around, when they had it over here on the school ground, I saw my kettle. They'd bored a hole in it and bolted it to the floor. Ruined a plumb good kettle."

Drifting along on the current of Delano's story, it was hard for Jennings to think anything had changed in Newfound, but he knew better. Newfound *had* changed; *he* had changed. And now Jennings wondered if Delano didn't think him a little foolish too for wanting the old Shelton house, like the people who bored a hole in the iron kettle. And he wondered if Delano might not be right.

5

This was going to be awkward.

Jennings had driven into Jewell Hill to see if he could find out when Mr. and Mrs. Shelton would be out of their old log house down by the lake, the one he'd bought from the Corps of Engineers. "Come in," Hilliard Shelton said, without looking up from his desk, when Jennings tapped lightly at the door of Hilliard's real estate office. Jennings studied Hilliard—how he'd changed over the years. How he'd rounded out and sat there now, a man in his fifties, wearing a white short-sleeved shirt, the pocket full of pens. Hilliard hardly resembled his father, old Greene Shelton, a man in his high seventies now, lean and hard still, with hawk-like eyes. Greene Shelton had vowed it would take a court order to move him off his place, and he was proving to be a man of his word. The forced removal of the Sheltons, from land taken for the lake, had been a running story in the *Cordell County Courier* for some months now. Hilliard had been quoted as favoring his parents' removal; he'd been trying to get them to move out of that old log house for years. They could come live with him in more comfortable circumstances, Hilliard had told a reporter.

Finally Hilliard looked up from a page of figures. He stared at Jennings, then smiled a wry smile. Hilliard had a small, almost feminine mouth. Put Jennings in mind of Phil Gramm, the Texas Senator, or Jesse Helms, the Senator from North Carolina. "Well, well, well!" Hilliard said. "The seldom seen and often heard about Mr. Jennings Wells. Perfessor Wells, I guess I ought to say. You still stomping out ignorance at that college over in Virginia?"

"Well, no, Hilliard. I'm taking a little time off," Jennings said.

Hilliard motioned to a chair. "Seems to me I *did* hear somebody say you're back up on Newfound."

Jennings sat down. Hilliard hadn't changed, he thought. Always playing his cards close to his chest, seeming to know less than he actually did. Hilliard knew damn well that Jennings was back home. "I guess you know—I bought your Mama and Daddy's house down there by the lake."

"Heard that, too," Hilliard said, flipping a pen against the edge of his desk. "And wondered about it."

"There's no rush—" Jennings hesitated. This was awkward. "No rush at all. But I thought you might know when your Mama and Daddy would be out of that house."

"They'll be out before long," Hilliard said. He reached into the pocket of a blue blazer that hung on the back of his chair, found a cigarette, and lit it. "I reckon Papa'll have to hear the papers read, though," he said, blowing smoke, "before he'll leave."

Jennings felt uneasy, sitting here talking to his old adversary. Hilliard Shelton was the man he'd differed with repeatedly

27

over the years—about development, strip mining, the future of Cordell County. But differed with him from a distance—in the books he'd written, in articles and letters to the editor he'd sent to the *Cordell County Courier.* This was the man whose sister, Roseanne, he'd almost married. Would have married. But there'd been a long and painful breakup. Roseanne had gone north, then brought a child and left it with her parents, all those years ago. That time seemed to Jennings now like another country. Still, he felt uneasy, thinking of Roseanne, and even more uneasy in the realization that he was sounding like a landlord anxious to evict tenants.

Jennings watched Hilliard rub the sides of his nose beneath his glasses. "It's a little bit of a sticky situation," Hilliard said. "Nothing I can't handle, though. I've been trying to get Mama and Papa out of that old house for a long time, get them over to my place. Not been able to budge them till this new lake come in. I'll have them out before long."

"There's the boy, too. Buddy. Roseanne's boy. I've run into him," Jennings said.

"He's welcome to come, too—finish his school. As long as he understands he'll be living in my house. He's headstrong, that boy, Roseanne's boy. Headstrong, for sure."

The door opened and a short stout man in khaki pants, sweat-stained khaki shirt and baseball cap entered. Jennings studied the round face with its three-day reddish stubble—a kind of furtive, groundhog look.

"You know Cecil, here, I guess," Hilliard said.

"Cecil Pedigo. Yeah. We go way back." Jennings recollected the time he'd fought Cecil on the school ground. Once Cecil had stolen Jennings' clothes off a bush by a swimming hole on Ivy Creek.

"You fellers probably went to school together," Hilliard said.

Cecil tugged at the bill of his hat. "What little I went," he said.

Jennings noticed the lettering on Cecil's cap: Cordell County Sheriff's Dept. Cecil also carried a beeper on his belt.

"Thought you were off the force, Cecil, after the last election."

"I'll get back on, come another election," Cecil said.

"Maybe before that," Hilliard said, grinning. He turned in his green swivel chair and twirled his pen between his fingers.

"You think our new sheriff—who is it? Ratliff?—you think he's going to be indicted for dealing drugs?" Jennings asked.

"Prob'ly," Cecil said, grinning at Hilliard.

"He's still on the job," Hilliard said noncommitally. "And I want Ratliff on the job at least till he can read the papers to Papa, get him and Mama out of that old house."

Jennings watched Hilliard leaf through papers on his desk, then look up at Cecil. "Cecil, go out to the trailer park, see if you can fix the leak in number twelve." He handed Cecil a piece of paper and picked up another one. "Go by twenty-one, tell that no-account sonofabitch Jack Price if I don't have my rent by the fifth, I'm sending the sheriff to put *him* out!"

Cecil winked at Jennings. "Jack, he'll pay after he sells his marijuana crop."

Hilliard handed Cecil another piece of paper. "You tell him what I said. And go by Troy's and see if he's got them air conditioners ready."

Turning to leave, Cecil said to Jennings, "See you in the funny papers."

Summoning up all his wit, Jennings thought. Jennings rose to leave, too, but Hilliard motioned for him to stay.

29

"Yeah, it may take a week or two," Hilliard said. "But I'll have Mama and Papa out of that house. What I was wondering, what do you want with that old house? You can't hardly get your money out of it, can you?"

"I'm not interested in getting my money out of it," Jennings said. "It's just that—I bought your Daddy's old house, I guess, just so I could keep it here in the county. The old house seems to stand for everything Cordell County used to be, before the roads came."

Jennings watched Hilliard look at him, first with disbelief, then with a condescending little smile, as if he were talking to the feeble-minded. Jennings hated that smile.

"Perfessor Wells must be into this 'heritage' business," Hilliard said. "I saw one of your little articles in the paper awhile back."

"Yeah. It has to do with that," Jennings said. "I bought your Daddy's old house so we'd have something to help us remember how it used to be here in Cordell County." He thought of telling Hilliard that the whole county struck him as being like somebody who'd had a blow to the head and couldn't remember who they were. But he thought better.

"Any money in heritage?" Hilliard asked, grinning as he doodled on a piece of paper with his pen.

"I guess not," Jennings said.

"I've never been interested in getting into anything that wouldn't pay, somehow."

He said it proudly, Jennings thought. "That's your way, all right, Hilliard," he said. He aimed to be agreeable and leave as quickly as he could.

"You always did have ideas, Perfessor Wells," Hilliard said. "That's been your trouble."

30

"Ideas. Yeah. They'll get a feller into trouble, all right, Hilliard. Is that how you've kept out of trouble, Hilliard?"

And immediately he regretted having said that.

But Hilliard either missed or ignored the dig. "Why, I was raised up in that old house," Hilliard said.

He was just ignoring it, Jennings thought. Always seeming dumber than he was. "I know you were," Jennings said. "That's why I thought maybe you'd want it."

"Hell, no! I wouldn't give you a nickel for that old house."

"Don't you like to remember growing up in it?" Jennings asked.

"No, sir. All I remember is how cold and drafty it was. I was glad to get out of it, and I did, soon as I could." He seemed for a minute to be genuinely puzzled by Jennings. "Me and you, we've always differed. It looks to me like you're headed in the wrong direction, going backwards instead of forwards. What's the sense in going backwards?"

Jennings studied Hilliard. He'd often wondered how people like old Mr. and Mrs. Shelton could produce a son like Hilliard, so different from them, so different from his sister Roseanne. He knew Hilliard wasn't a bad man, not somebody who rolled out of bed every morning thinking what evil thing he could do that day. Obviously, Hilliard was proud of what he'd amounted to, starting out poor, making some money in timber and coal, now in real estate. He'd become one of Cordell County's advocates for progress, serving on boards and committees. And here he sat, with all the certificates of appreciation, photos, and awards on the wall behind him. Jennings noticed he'd even won a conservation award. A tub thumper for strip mining wins the conservation award! Jennings smiled. "You're right, Hilliard. We differ."

"We've sucked the hind tit here in Cordell County too long," Hilliard said. "Didn't even get decent roads in here till 1969. You know that."

"We got the roads to haul out coal," Jennings said. "You know that better than anybody, Hilliard."

Hilliard looked almost puzzled. "Couldn't get the coal out without the roads," he said.

Jennings grinned. He thought of a New Jersey state legislator and liquor store owner he'd read about somewhere, a man who was asked to refrain from voting on some liquor legislation because it would constitute a conflict of interest. "How does that conflict with my interest?" the man had asked. Hilliard saw things that way. And there were thousands like him, Jennings knew. Hilliard was just a mountain version of that illusion, the self-made man, the kind of man who wants to forget where he came from, forget the GI Bill that bootstrapped him, forget that the roads were built because people in a board room in Pittsburgh decided it was time to go after the coal in Cordell County, coal their corporation had held rights to before Hilliard was born. It was coincidence as much as anything that put Hilliard where he was. There was no such thing as a self-made man. It was convenient, though, to think of oneself that way. Jennings guessed they'd been brought up to think that way. "We've got roads, but now half the county's torn up," Jennings said.

"We're still better off than before," Hilliard said.

"A few people may be better off. You sure are," Jennings said.

"Damn right. I was born poor, and I'm not ashamed of it. But I didn't stay poor. And I would've turned over ever foot of land in Cordell County—if that's what it took. Besides, it don't hurt land to strip mine it," Hilliard said. "Not in the long run. I've said it before and I still believe it."

Jennings had heard this before, and still he couldn't believe he was hearing it. "What's scary, Hilliard, is you probably *do* believe it."

"Once you get the coal out, see, you can put the land back with a better contour. Make it good for something. You can raise cattle on land that's been stripped and then contoured right, where before it was so steep a goat'd fall off of it!"

"What about water, Hilliard?"

"We've got plenty of water."

Jennings shook his head. "Acid water. Polluted water. Cordell County's water's in bad shape, Hilliard, and you know it. It's making people sick. We don't have the sewage system for this much development."

"We've got good water . . . and plenty of it," Hilliard maintained. "Why, if I had my way, every foot of land in Cordell County'd be flat as a pool table. Airports. Once the land has been leveled, you can put an airport on a strip mine site. I think we may be able to get one."

"If one can be got, you'll probably get it for us, Hilliard," Jennings said. "And how about another landfill? They're pretty popular nowadays. Maybe you can do deals and get us two or three landfills!"

His elbows propped on his desk, Hilliard made a tent with his fingers. "Me and you differs on lots of things, but we agree about one thing. We both love this place."

Jennings could see that Hilliard was almost choked with emotion. And he knew that, in his way, Hilliard did love Cordell County. Loved the country. He was the kind of man who'd display a bumper sticker that said, "Burning my flag may be hazardous to your health." And did, on a Cadillac.

"But how can you love a place and still want to see it cut up

33

and abused?" Jennings asked. "If you love your dog, you don't kick it, do you? If you love a woman, you don't mistreat her, do you?"

"What's a woman got to do with it?" Hilliard asked.

Sometimes, Jennings thought, Hilliard just didn't get it. Maybe he was as dumb as he sometimes seemed. He had a particular kind of mind, Hilliard. He could set his mind on something, and keep it there. But his mind wouldn't leap. It took hold and hung on.

"Listen," Hilliard said, "I knew you're back home. I been meaning to get up there on Newfound and talk to you. Here's the deal: like I said, me and you, we differ. Always have. But I can differ with a man and still do business with him."

A coal truck rumbled by outside.

"Business?" Jennings said.

Hilliard smiled slyly. "This lake coming in and all, I need a man like you—educated—to help me out here in the county. A man that can handle paper work, talk to people, do deals." Hilliard motioned to the door Cecil had left through. "You take Cecil, there's just certain things Cecil can do."

Jennings shook his head. "I'm not looking for work, Hilliard!"

"Thought you might be. Well, you think about it. Feller like you—you know this county, know the people, how they think." Hilliard picked up a sheaf of papers and envelopes. "Land." He leaned forward toward Jennings. "You could put together parcels of land."

As Jennings studied him, Hilliard's eyes brightened. "Heritage Acres! How's that sound?"

"It's not for me, Hilliard."

"For all I know," Hilliard said, running the tip of his tongue across his lower lip, "you might be interested in selling your place there on Newfound."

34

"No."

"Or selling off a parcel. A few tracts. Putting in some trailers or little houses. All kinds of ways to go at it. Bring yourself a nice little monthly income."

"Not interested, Hilliard."

"You never know. You think about it."

"Hilliard, I didn't come home to go to work for you, or go into real estate. I don't even know that I've come home—for good. I'm just trying something." He shook his head. "Here we are, having the same argument we had twenty-five years ago."

"Thought maybe you'd smartened up since then," Hilliard said.

"Ever hear from your sister?" Jennings asked.

"Roseanne. No, I don't hear from her." Hilliard seemed reluctant to elaborate. But then he said: "Hell, even Roseanne knew back then I was right about the roads. She sided with me—remember?"

Jennings stood to go. "Yeah, I remember. Well, like I said, no rush about the house."

"Me and you can do business," Hilliard said.

Jennings moved toward the door. "Hilliard," he said, "I won't be working for you, or with you. I'm probably just going to make trouble for you."

"Trouble?" Hilliard smiled his little pucker-mouthed smile. "You won't make trouble for *me*!" He looked at Jennings, then said: "You mean them books you wrote? Them little articles you're always putting in the paper? They don't bother me! That stuff—it may be right, somewheres else. It may be right in your house. But not in my house."

What an odd mind Hilliard had. Damned quirky. "That's curious, Hilliard. I thought if something was true, it was true everywhere!"

"Not in my house," Hilliard muttered.

Shaking his head, Jennings took another step toward the door.

"You go ahead, *say* anything you want to. Just—"

"Thanks, Hilliard," Jennings said. "But I didn't know I had to have your permission."

Hilliard came from behind his desk. "No, sir, you won't make trouble for me, Mr. Perfessor Wells. Least, nothing I won't know how to handle."

That's Hilliard, Jennings thought. Prides himself on *handling* things. "Take care, Hilliard."

"No, *you* take care!" Hilliard said, in a tone that startled Jennings. "Something I'd like to know. Perfessor Wells is coming home! How in the hell can you even call this place home—if you've not lived here for twenty-five years? What right do you have to call Cordell County home? It's people who've lived here, and built it up—I've *lived* here, Mr. Perfessor! You've not."

Jennings had known ten minutes ago he'd stayed too long. "It's been about the same talking to you, Hilliard."

"Yeah, you go on and *say* anything you want to," Hilliard repeated. "Just watch what you *do!*"

Driving out of Jewell Hill, back toward Newfound, Jennings imagined how the county seat looked to Hilliard. A new fast food place—Druther's. A new shirt factory at the edge of town. Onward, upward.

6

He stopped by The Trading Post later that afternoon, logged some time with the boys on the loafers bench. Delano Crumm was finishing an old joke just as Jennings walked over and sat down. "So he held a pistol on this poverty worker and made him drink white liquor out of that fruit jar. That poverty worker gagged and gasped for breath. Then he handed the pistol to the poverty worker and said, 'Now, you hold the gun on me while I take a drink'!" Delano laughed, looked up, and winked at Jennings. "I think I've drunk some of that liquor," Jennings said.

While they were sitting there talking, arranging to dismantle the old Shelton house, Cecil Pedigo drove up in his old brown Pontiac. He must have finished running errands for Hilliard.

"Here comes Deputy Dawg," Delano said.

"With his beeper," Wiley Woolford said. "Still wearing his deputy hat, and him not been a deputy since last election."

Two fishing rods stuck up in the back seat of Cecil's Pontiac.

As Cecil shuffled up, making a crunching noise in the gravel, Wiley Woolford said, "Fish biting, Cecil?"

"Just little devils," Cecil said. Jennings nodded to Cecil and watched as Cecil straightend a board laid across two cinder blocks and sat down on it. "Bet I caught a hunnert croppies—nothing but eyes and gills."

"It'll take awhile before fish in this here new lake gets any size on 'em," Dee Rhodommer said.

"Only thing I snagged any size here lately," Cecil said, "was a damned old needle-nose garfish. I hate them sumbitches. Tuck and drove a stick straight up and down between his jaws. Throwed him back in. He won't be jerking nobody else's bobber under." Cecil pulled out a pocketknife and began to cut a notch in the board he sat on. "I'm gonna go after squirrels 'stead of fish."

"Squirrel season's not open yet, is it, boys?" Delano Crumm said, looking around at Wiley and Dee and Jennings.

"I don't give a rat's ass," Cecil said. "Game warden won't write me up. I used to deputy with him. I got a hunnert and forty-seven last year."

"Squirrels?" Wiley Woolford said.

"Going for two hunnert this year. Two hunnert—if I have to kill the last squirrel in Cordell County."

"You'd do it, too, wouldn't you, Cecil?" Dee Rhodommer said.

"Hell, yes."

A few minutes later, while they were still sitting there talking, Cecil got a call on his beeper.

"Look out!" Delano Crumm said, throwing up his hands in mock alarm. "Cecil's starting to beep!"

Cecil got up, walked over to his car, leaned against it, and answered the beeper.

"Sure are getting modern here in Cordell County," Wiley Woolford said.

Cecil got in his car and drove off.

"Cecil still thinks he's a deputy," Dee Rhodommer said to Jennings.

"You heard about Cecil and the FBI, didn't you, Jennings," Delano said.

"No, what?"

Delano laughed in anticipation of his own story. "He told it on hisself, sitting right there where he was sitting a minute ago. Said he was with Sammy Porter and Buck Fraley and that bunch, playing poker at Buck's in Jewell Hill one Saturday here a year or two ago. Buck, he'd set out a round or two, was back in the kitchen on the telephone a long time. First thing they knowed there's three state police cars in front of the house, and then two more pulled up, with them blue lights a-whirling. Big knock come to the door and Cecil opened it, he said, and there stood three or four smokies, big mothers, wanting to know did Buck Fraley live there.

"Cecil and them others said, sure. It was Buck's place. Right about then Buck come out wanting to know what was going on. Well, after they made sure he was Buck Fraley, this smoky asked him—Did you call to the White House and make a threat on the President's life? Buck reckoned he might have, it was a free country, wasn't it?

"Well, they arrested Buck right there, hauled him off. Then some of the other smokies stayed there and questioned old Cecil and Sammy and whoever else it was there playing cards. Did any of them hear Buck call the White House and threaten to kill the President? Did Buck have a history of doing that sort of thing? Had Buck ever pulled anything like that before? No,

39

they hadn't heard Buck call. As far as they knowed, Buck never had done anything like that."

"They asked, 'Did Buck have any previous history of making violent threats?' " Dee Rhodommer said. "No, not that Cecil or any of them knowed."

"Asked about Buck's politics, too," Wiley Woolford recollected. "Cecil said, why, as far as he knowed, Buck never had even voted."

Delano winked at Jennings. "FBI come in on it, and talked to Cecil three times after that, what Cecil said. Said they'd come, two FBI men together, and take out their notebooks and talk to Cecil. Something was wrong, they said, something was missing. Could Cecil think of *anything* Buck Fraley'd ever done that would make Cecil think he was capable of threatening to kill the President?"

"Cecil couldn't think of a thing. Buck was just old Buck. Always had been. One of the boys."

"They come and talked to Cecil a second time," Wiley said.

"Three times all together," Dee said.

"Cecil said he told them that second time he thought they were barking up the wrong tree," Delano said. "He didn't care if they did have Buck down at the state hospital running tests on him. Buck wasn't crazy. Buck never had had sense enough to go crazy. Well, still and all, they wished Cecil'd give the whole thing some more thought, think back, and they'd be talking to him again. Well, sir, when they come that third time Cecil said he had thought about it and maybe he had thought of something. He did recollect how old Buck'd get something on his mind sometimes, get to worrying about it, and he usually liked to go right to the top to get something done about it. Like when they were strip mining over there around Powderly and tore the road up and Buck couldn't get anything done about it, and he'd get it on his mind, especially in bad weather, and for awhile there he'd call the Governor's Mansion, like at two or three in the morning.

"Then there was the time, Cecil told 'em, that Buck had trouble with his foreman at the plant. Buck'd got laid off, and he went back down to the plant to talk to the foreman, foreman wouldn't talk to him, so Buck went out to his truck, got his chain saw, and tried to saw through the door to get to the foreman. Hit something metal, broke the chain, chain flew back in his face—left that scar. Cecil said he reckoned that *would* be something of a violent nature."

"He set right here and told it on hisself," Wiley Woolford said.

"It's the tom truth," Dee Rhodommer said to Jennings.

Delano lit his pipe and puffed on it. "Said them FBI men just set there looking at him for the longest time. Said they'd been asking Cecil over and over did Buck Fraley have any history of threats and violence. Did it take Cecil a week to remember that Buck had a habit of threatening the governor, or that he'd tried to kill his foreman with a chain saw?—Jesus! They thought maybe Cecil was as crazy as Buck."

"What'd Cecil say to that?" Jennings asked.

"Cecil said he told 'em he didn't know for a fact that Buck ever threatened the governor when he called up there. Buck was probably just trying to get the road fixed."

"Cecil—he's told that here two or three times," Wiley said. "He set right here and said Buck's going after his foreman with that chain saw, maybe that was violent, but in the end Buck didn't hurt anybody but hisself. You've heard it, ain't you, Delano?"

Delano grinned. "Cecil's got this notion—violence is when

41

somebody you don't know mugs you, or once he said violence was when they blow up women and younguns in some foreign country."

"When people know one another," Dee said, "like Buck knowing his foreman, Cecil says that's not violence, because you know what it's all about."

"Cecil still argues that. What do you think, Jennings?"

"I think somebody who'd jam a stick straight up and down in a fish's mouth and turn it back in the water—I think anybody who'd do that might have a bit of a blind spot when it comes to violence," Jennings said.

"Or that'd set right here and say he'd kill the last squirrel in Cordell County," Dee said. "Any fool knows you've got to leave some for seed."

"I think Cecil's dumb as a coal bucket—what I think," Wiley said.

"I do too," Delano said. "But you don't want Cecil mad at you. He'd just as soon cut you as not—knock you in the head. He's sneaky. That whole push of Pedigos is like that. But I'll have to admit, there's lots of things that's goes on around here, when you get right down to it, they're violent. But we don't pay much attention to 'em. I've studied on it. You take, when old Mr. and Mrs. Sinclair got shot and killed in their little store, like happened here awhile back, and it turns out to be some escaped convict from Michigan, wearing a ski mask, and he didn't know them from Adam—recollect how tore up people got? How scared everybody got there for a while? But when J.R. Hall got hopped up and went over to his ex-wife's trailer, busted in on her, and she told him not ever to come around her again, and he come right back the next night, roughed her up, and she blowed him away—now think how people took that? People knowed how long that had been going on, knowed J.R., knowed his wife. Most people just said J.R. needed killing.—I mean, there's violence, and then there's violence, if you know what I mean."

"Still it's all violence," Wiley said. "What do you think, Jennings?"

"You fellers bring up big subjects," Jennings said. "When are we gonna knock down the old Shelton house?"

7

He discovered he couldn't work in the house. Too hot. He moved table and typewriter out on the screened-in porch, but that proved breezeless, too. Finally, under the big maple in the front yard, he made a table from sawhorses and seasoned boards. He had worked there into the late afternoon when a blue Mercury came rolling up the drive ahead of a cloud of dust. The car whipped right up to the edge of the yard, the radio playing country music. As the door flew open, he caught the words "Mama, He's Crazy." A woman with crow-black hair, in jeans and an Outlaws tee shirt, got out and walked across the yard toward him. She left the car door hanging open, the radio playing.

"Heard you were home," she said, striding confidently.

"Hello," Jennings said. He started to get up, but before he could she popped down on the ground beside his makeshift table. Sitting cross-legged, she laid a blade of grass between her thumbs and blew on it.

At first he thought she must be some rural hophead, or some

mildly retarded child-woman allowed to run around the community unsupervised. But it was obvious she knew him—and from way back. Yet he had no idea who she was! Not for a long time. Only when she mentioned her brother Clyde and squirrel hunting did he realize this was one of the Livesay girls. Then he knew which Livesay girl.

This was Roma, the next to youngest. He remembered how, years ago—he'd been sixteen, maybe—he used to go squirrel hunting with her older brother Clyde. Once, while he waited there in the front yard at the Livesay place, his .22 in the crook of his arm, little Roma, her black hair done in dog ears, had sat on the porch steps just looking at him, and all the while, quite unselfconsciously—she might not have been quite school age at the time—her dress hiked over her thighs, her white cotton panties pushed to one side, she'd massaged her crotch and stared up at him as he stood waiting for her brother Clyde to come out of the house.

"R-Roma?" Jennings said.

"Well, yes, dummy! Who'd you think I was?" she said, and blew on the grass blade.

They talked awhile and she left, whipping the Mercury around at the edge of the yard, leaving Jennings sitting there dazed. He found it hard to pair his recollection of that little suntanned black-haired girl, her hand in her crotch, staring up at him, with this vivid woman in her mid-thirties who drove an old Mercury with such authority, and who proved so familiar with his career and accomplishments throughout all the years he'd been away, years when he hadn't given her a thought.

She came back the next afternoon, and the next, outrunning a dust cloud, whipping around at the edge of the yard and releas-

45

ing country music from the car radio like a flock of gaudy birds. By the third afternoon Jennings was glancing at his watch in anticipation of her arrival. They went in the house. While he made drinks, she straightened up the living room, declaring it a "hog waller."

They drank, talked. Roma found a station on the radio called The Beaver (she scorned WWJH, the Jewell Hill station) and sat cross-legged on the floor—wouldn't sit in a chair—her sun-tanned face framed by crow-black hair. Sometimes, he thought, she looked almost Incan.

She wanted him to like country music, filled him in on what he'd missed, apparently, since Lefty Frizell, Kitty Wells, and the death of Hank Williams, which was all he could remember when he'd claimed to know something about country music. She wanted to know what he thought about every song they listened to, couldn't see what was wrong with some of the songs he made fun of—songs she liked.

Some of the songs, he said, he found interesting—"Wild and Blue" and "I Don't Remember Loving You"—because they presented love as a pathological state.

What didn't he like? she wanted to know.

He didn't like dumb puns—"The only thing I can count on now is my fingers." Any song about a deck of cards. Any here-I-am-in-my-cups-again song.

How come?

Because, Jennings said, he always wanted to say to the singer: You might not be so depressed if you'd lighten up on the booze.

But there was a lot of truth in some of those old drinking songs, Roma thought.

Nah! Jennings said a moratorium ought to be declared on them—and on truck-driving, big-wheels-rolling songs.

46

Roma said Jennings was just a snob.

No, there just weren't many good songs. Take, for instance, all those uxorious I-love-only-you songs.

Did Jennings mean songs where the man was pussy-whipped? Roma wanted to know.

He wouldn't put it just that way, Jennings said, startled. He thought "uxorious" . . . .

She looked up at him, mischief in her eyes. She had been to school, too. Learned some words. Words like *uxorious*. It was the kind of word she liked to learn—and then not say!

Jennings took the glass from her hand, to freshen her drink. He liked this woman, this Roma.

If he was going to say uxorious, he might just as well go ahead and say pussy-whipped, Roma declared.

Whatever. Also, he despised all those thank-god-I'm just a-common-man-in-a-common-van songs, glad-I'm-so-dumb-because-highbrow-people-are-crazy songs.

That proved it! Jennings was just a snob and a highbrow, Roma said. A hit dog hollering.

Not so, Jennings argued. All lowbrows weren't sensible, all highbrows weren't insane. Mental wards were full of lowbrow crazies, more so than with highbrows—because there were more lowbrows to start with!

What else? she wanted to know. What else didn't he like?

Jennings handed her drink back to her. He didn't like poor-lovers-stay-together-but-let-them-get-a-two-story-house-and-the-marriage-falls-to-pieces songs.

Sometimes that's the way it is, Roma believed. In her case, though, she'd been poor and the marriage still fell apart—twice! What performers did he like?

He sort of liked Anne Murray.

Roma poked a finger into her mouth, as if to induce vomiting. She could see they weren't ready to dance without stepping on one another's feet!

Jennings guessed not. But he thought Roma sounded a little like Anne Murray, because Roma's talk was always right on the edge of song.

Roma didn't want to argue about Anne Murray.

Yes, she did. She loved to argue, Jennings told her.

Roma smiled.

Jennings found himself liking to say things that made her smile, and he was pretty good at it.

Roma looked around the room at the stacks of books he'd carried in from the car and hadn't yet shelved. "You've been through the books, sure enough."

Jennings said he couldn't help it if he'd been advantaged by his upbringing.

She smiled.

Each time she left, Jennings sat in a mood that lingered like perfume. He didn't know what to make of her. He had known her, at least known about her, since she was a child. Had known her parents, grandparents, brothers and sisters. So he should have understood her easily. But he didn't. In fact, she made him feel a little shy and awkward because he *did* remember her as a little girl, and had never known her as the woman she was now.

She'd been to school, all right. Had a post-graduate degree and worked now in the Cordell County Department of Social Services. Had been married—twice. And lived in a neat frame house on the Sugar Creek Road. She'd read all his books, liked some better than others. (So did he!) But she didn't care to elaborate. Her habit of mind, it seemed, was to take something complex and go straight to the heart of it, sum it up, and move on. He tended to stay with a matter, unpack it, examine every aspect of it, then put it all back together in some different arrangement. She made him feel phony when he did this. She came across to him as more direct, to the point of bluntness, and somehow freer, not only in what she thought and said but even in her movements. The way she exited her Mercury, or crossed to his worktable and sat down. So matter-of-fact and uncomplicated. But she wasn't simple. She was bright. How much of her was bright bluff? He couldn't be sure. All he knew was that sometimes he had the feeling she was saying a lot less than she might have. . . . Maybe she was exactly as she presented herself: someone who wanted to be able to say all sorts of things, and then not say them!

Whatever. But he hadn't come across a pleasanter puzzle than Roma in. . . . well, not ever.

8

As he came into view of it, just for an instant, Jennings Wells thought he saw someone quickly close the front door of the old Shelton house. But there couldn't be anybody in the old house now. Shouldn't be. Mr. and Mrs. Shelton had been moved out two or three days now, and the boy who lived with them, Buddy, their grandchild, Roseanne's boy, surely had gone with them.

Jennings pulled to a stop at the edge of the yard, turned off the ignition, and reached for his camera on the seat beside him. He wanted photos of the house from every angle. Even though every log in the old two-story house would be numbered before it was dismantled, he wanted photographs of the house on its original site. And if there were any doubt, as they re-assembled the house, he could check the photographs to make sure it was put back together just as it had been. Odd, how he'd thought he saw that door swing to.

Jennings was standing beside his car framing the old log house in the view finder, his eye right on the front door, when the door opened again. He looked up and lowered the camera as the boy stepped out holding two large oval picture frames against his chest. "Buddy?" Jennings said. He'd got to know the boy since he'd been back in Newfound. He'd first seen Buddy at The Trading Post. Later the boy had come around asking to do odd jobs for cash.

Holding the picture frames close to his body, the boy stepped out the door onto the porch. "What are you doing?" he said.

Buddy stood there defiantly, sandy-haired, slight, in jeans and a denim shirt. Small for fifteen or sixteen, which was how old he had to be, Jennings thought, remembering when the boy's mother, Roseanne Shelton, left Newfound. "Buddy?" Jennings Wells said again.

"What are you doing?" the boy repeated.

Jennings Wells stepped toward the porch. "What say, Buddy? Didn't expect to run into you here. Thought you'd be gone with your Grandma and Grandpa Shelton."

"What are you taking pictures for?" the boy asked.

Jennings strode on over to the porch steps and stood looking up at the boy. "I wanted some pictures of the place just the way it always looked before the logs are numbered."

"Numbered?"

"Yeah, you always number the logs so you don't get them mixed up after you take them apart."

"Apart?" The boy walked on out to the edge of the porch. "You can't take this house apart!"

"I bought this house, Buddy," Jennings said. "Didn't anybody tell you?" He motioned to the outbuildings. "The crib and barn, and the springhouse, they go to a museum over in Tennessee. I got the house from the Army Corps of Engineers. Would have got the other buildings too if I'd known in time. You got some pictures there?"

51

The boy stepped off the porch onto the steps. "You're not taking this house apart!"

"Buddy, it belongs to the Army Corps of Engineers. Did, till I bought it."

Now the boy moved back up the steps onto the porch again, as if defending the house. "This is my house!" he said.

"Now, Buddy. These buildings have been sold. I've just been waiting for your Grandpa and Grandma Shelton to move out, so . . . . Your Grandma and Grandpa Shelton, they've been moved over to your Uncle Hilliard's, what, three or four days now, haven't they?"

"*I've* not moved out!" the boy said.

"Well, you're supposed to be," Jennings said. "Supposed to be in school, too."

"Not any school today—it's Saturday."

"Oh. That's right, so it is."

"You don't even know what day it is!"

Jennings stood looking at the boy, who stared defiantly, then finally looked down at the ground. Jennings had already been talking to the boy about school, and had refused to let the boy work for him during school hours. "What did you think to do—just sit back on your thumb, and live on here with the hoot owls?"

"I'm not going to Hilliard's," Buddy said. "That big-butt!— Not going to Cordell County High School, either!"

"You're thinking to be a Henry, aren't you?" Jennings said, recalling a recent afternoon when Buddy had mowed branch banks for him and talked about his plans to live in the woods. Jennings had told Buddy he sounded like Henry Thoreau and started calling him Henry, something the boy resented.

"Don't start in on that," Buddy said. "I'm Buddy."

"I'm just taking the house a little ways," Jennings said. "Going

52

to put it back together again, down at my place. A couple of fellers are coming over here in a little while to mark the logs and start taking them down."

"No!" Buddy said.

"Yeah. You're always wanting to work for me—you can help those fellers take the house down, and after they . . . ."

"I want this house to be here!" Buddy said, stomping his foot on the porch.

". . . and after they haul the logs over to my place, you can help them put it back together.—Okay?"

Buddy stood shaking his head from side to side.

Jennings thought he caught a resemblance—something in the eyes—between this boy and his mother, Roseanne. "Your Grandma and Grandpa Shelton know you're still over here?"

Buddy stood rooted and didn't answer.

"They're gonna be uneasy about you—about where you are," Jennings said. "You come on, I'll drive you down there."

"I told you, I'm not going to Hilliard's!"

Jennings felt sorry for the boy. He'd known for years now that Roseanne Shelton had left the boy with her parents when Buddy was no more than two or three years old. But Jennings had been away all the years and hadn't seen the boy until he came back home this time and Buddy had come around asking to do jobs around the run-down homeplace. He was a likeable kid, and a good worker, and he was Roseanne's boy. Jennings was inclined to be patient with him. "If it's the house you're worried about," Jennings said, sitting down on the porch steps, "like I said—I'm just moving it. In a little while, it'll be just like it is now—only it'll be down at my house."

"What do you want it for, anyway?" Buddy asked.

Jennings considered the question, realizing it might seem odd that he would want to buy an old two-story log house when he already had his Grandfather and Grandmother Wells' house, the house his mother and father had also lived in the last twenty years of their lives. A big frame I-house, one of the best homes in Newfound. He guessed—no, he was sure—he wanted to save the old Shelton house, one of the oldest authentic log homes in Cordell County, maybe in the whole end of the state. It was the house Roseanne Shelton grew up in, and while he realized Roseanne, wherever she was, wasn't interested in the house, and certainly her booster brother Hilliard wasn't, well, Jennings did want to save it. "If I move the house down to my place," he told Buddy, "that'll be better than if it was taken over to Silver City, or some place like that, and set up so somebody dressed up like a hillbilly, with a gun and dog and jug, shoots 'revenoors'—while a crowd stands gawking. Fake shoot-outs to draw crowds.—Don't you think?"

"Best thing is, if it stays right where it is," Buddy said.

"I'm saving the house," Jennings said, glancing up at Buddy on the porch.

The boy's eyes flashed. "You're tearing it down!"

"Sure. But I'm keeping it here. In Newfound." Jennings got up from the porch steps, walked out into the yard, turned, and snapped a photo of Buddy standing on the porch. "If I hadn't got it, the Corps would have sold it, just like they did the barn and crib and springhouse. They don't want any buildings on the land around the lake." He snapped several shots of the corner notchings at both ends of the house.

Buddy came down the steps and laid his picture frames on the porch. He shook his head. Jennings heard him mumble again: "No."

"Yes!" Jennings said, as he walked to the side of the house, stepped back, and snapped a photo. "Tell you what, we'll drive over to that museum sometime, when the barn's put back together, and the crib and the springhouse. You can see them over there. Like I said, I'm just glad I got the house. I like this old house the same as you. You'll be coming over to my place, like you've been doing, to do jobs for me. This house will be right there."

Buddy followed Jennings around the house still shaking his head.

Jennings was at the back of the house still arguing with Buddy when he heard a car coming up the wagon road. That would be Delano, Wiley Woolford and Dee Rhodommer, the fellows he'd hired to come mark the logs and start dismantling the house. But as the car came closer, he thought he recognized the throaty muffler. And when it pulled up out front and he heard the car radio playing country music, he knew before he came from behind the house that it was Roma.

She came around the car in faded jeans and a pink shirt, brushing her black hair out of her eyes. "Hi! I drove over to your house before I remembered you said you'd probably be down here."

Jennings watched her look first from him to Buddy, then back to him. He could tell she sensed something. "If you fellers are fixing to fight, don't mind me," she said, and turned as if to go back to her old blue Mercury.

"Well, Henry here . . ." Jennings said.

"My name's Buddy. I've told you a hundred times."

"I call him Henry because he wants to live in the woods, like Henry Thoreau," Jennings explained.

"He's tearing my house down!" Buddy said.

Jennings walked Roma back to the far side of her car, and steadying his camera on its top, stood there snapping more photos. "Think you could talk to him, Roma?" he said quietly. "I thought he'd gone with Mr. and Mrs. Shelton. Then found him still here awhile ago, thinking to live on here by himself, I reckon."

Roma called across the yard to Buddy. "You better go on over to your Uncle Hilliard's, Punkin. Stay with your Grandpa and Grandma."

"And get back in school," Jennings said, coming back into the yard. "Instead of growing up like a weed! Today's Saturday, but I bet you weren't in school yesterday, or the day before, either."

Buddy crossed to the woodpile at the edge of the yard and sat down on a block of wood. He picked up a stick and started beating the ground with it. "I'm not going to live at Hilliard's, and I'm not going back to Cordell County High School!"

Jennings looked at Roma, who smiled. "How do I get into these situations? Listen, about yesterday. . . ."

"Hey, Jennings," Buddy said. He stopped beating the ground with the stick and looked up, as if something had occurred to him. "How about letting me have about—fifty dollars."

Jennings looked at Roma in mock astonishment. "I never took you to raise, Henry."

"I mean, lend it to me. Pay you back. Or else, work it out."

"You don't need fifty dollars, Henry," Jennings said. "You need to go on over to your Uncle Hilliard's, with your Grandma and Grandpa."

Roma leaned against Jennings. "It *is* best if you stay with your Grandma and Grandpa, Punkin," she said.

"And get back in school," Jennings repeated.

Buddy got up from the block of wood and walked toward them. "I need to borrow about fifty dollars."

"You're crazy, Henry," Jennings said. "If it was your Grandpa

Shelton talking, he'd say you need to be bored for holler-head!
Now, why do you need fifty dollars all of a sudden?"

"I could get a few things . . . groceries . . . stuff I need."

"To live in the woods, right, Henry?" Jennings said.

"Somewheres." Buddy walked right in front of Jennings and
Roma and stood with his thumbs hooked in the pockets of his
jeans. "Give me twenty dollars now and I'll go start mowing the
rest of that branch bank."

Jennings saw an opportunity to get Buddy moving. He took
out his wallet, fished out a twenty-dollar bill, and held it out to
Buddy. "Then go to it."

As Buddy reached out for the money, Jennings pulled the bill
back. "And then go on over to Hilliard's—all right?"

Buddy reached for the money without answering.

"All right?" Jennings repeated.

"All right," Buddy said finally. He took the money, pocketed
it, and walked to the porch and picked up the oval picture
frames. "But I'll just go see Grandma and Grandpa, I don't aim
to stay!" he said. He looked down at the old picture frames.
"Haulers went off and left these when they hauled stuff over to
Hilliard's. This here's my great Grandpa and Grandma."

"You want me to drive you over there, Henry?" Jennings said.
"I will. Or maybe Roma will."

"I'll walk. I want to."

Jennings stood there with Roma, beside their cars, watching
the boy walk down the wagon road with his framed pictures.

"I feel so sorry for him," Roma said. "He's lived in this house
all his life. Now he has to leave it, and he blames his Uncle
Hilliard."

"Maybe so, but he blames me too," Jennings said.

"It's more his Uncle Hilliard," Roma said, propping her elbows

57

on the hood of her blue Mercury. "Hilliard's part of the reason he hates school so much, too—Hilliard being head of the school board. Oh, did you know Hilliard's pushing to close the old Kingdom School?"

"I read about it," Jennings said.

He was leaning against Roma's car, talking, when Delano Crumm, Wiley Woolford, and Dee Rhodommer came up the wagon road in an old red Chevrolet pickup, to mark the logs and start taking the house apart. Jennings made a few more photos, angles suggested by Roma, and they decided to leave the men to their work. He was still thinking about the boy as they got into their cars. "I feel sorry for the boy too," he said to Roma. "But what can I do?"

He stood a minute by her car after Roma had slid under the wheel and started the Mercury. Her radio came on the country station with the turn of the ignition key. Jennings looked down at her and grinned. "I just seem to keep hitting one snag after another. First you, now this boy! I tell you, this trying to come home—it's not turning out to be what I thought it'd be."

Roma cocked her head and looked up at him through the open car window. "Want me to back off?"

"You'd better not! Come on down to the house," he said, and got into his car.

9

Roma drove ahead of him back to the house and was already inside, straightening up, when he pulled his car up behind hers. When he stepped inside, he could hear her mumbling to herself as she plumped pillows and cushions and stacked books. "Bookworm . . . humped up over that typewriter, pecking away." Turning to him, she said, "You probably meant what you said up there at the Shelton house awhile ago—about my being a snag you'd struck. Probably just as soon I'd stay away."

"Sit down, Roma." They were already into their routine, he knew. "You know I was kidding." He handed her a bourbon-and-water. "But it's true," he said, making another for himself, "when I came home, I never figured on you!"

"Or Buddy," she said, and sat down in front of him, cross-legged on the floor.

"Or Buddy.—I was thinking, driving back down here, when you rolled up out front there that first time, I have to admit . . ."

Roma sipped her drink and smiled, remembering. "And just popped down and started talking about everybody . . ."

"I have to tell you, for awhile there, I didn't . . ."

"I could tell, you didn't have a clue, Jennings Wells!"

"In my own defense," Jennings said, "I hadn't been back to Newfound, except just in and out for a day or two, for years. When you drove up here and started rattling on, like we went way back together, I kept trying to figure . . ."

"Trying to figure, who on God's earth *is* this madwoman? I could tell! And it served you right. You should've remembered."

Jennings reached down and brushed her hair from the right side of her face. "I thought, Roma? Is this little Roma? Who used to sit on the steps, her hair done up in dog ears, all those years ago, before I went off to school, when I'd come over to go hunting with her brother? I couldn't believe it."

"Well, I remembered you," Roma said, and sipped her drink. "In an old Army jacket, carrying a rifle, waiting for my brother to come out of the house."

Jennings laughed. "I've still not lived it down. After you left, that first day. I just kept sitting there at that table, wondering . . ."

"I could tell! I just wanted to see if you'd remember. Because I remembered you—remember when Clyde went into the Navy and you went off to school—when you finished. When you came back and taught school in Cordell County a year or two . . ."

"Yeah, two."

"Then you went back to school again. Next thing I knew, you were teaching in a college, over in Virginia. But you still came back to Newfound lots, back when . . ."

"Oh, practically every weekend, back then. Vacations, summers. When Mom and Dad were still living."

Roma gave him a sly look. "And when you and Roseanne Shelton were going together."

"You do remember a lot, don't you, Roma?"

"Everybody remembers when she was the star at the Rocky Top Festival. I was up in high school by then. That was about all us girls ever talked about—you and Roseanne Shelton."

"Well, that never . . ." He didn't quite know what he should say.

Roma said, "We thought you all were just like a Lord and Lady in one of those old ballads you all would sing at the Rocky Top Festival."

"That was a good thing—Rocky Top. But it played out. Roseanne went on the road with a band. Everything just played out."

"Next thing I knew," Roma said, "you were writing books. That one about the Rocky Top Festival, and . . ."

"I guess you don't much like my books, do you, Roma?"

"I never said that! What makes you think that?"

"Well, they made a lot of people around here mad because I criticized strip mining, and the way things have changed. I just thought . . ."

"Didn't make me mad," Roma said. "You told the truth! *How America Came to Cordell County.* That's a good book! I've read every one of them. Oh, I've kept up with you, Jennings Wells!"

Jennings took her empty glass from her hand. "Now that I'm back home, I'm going to keep up with you," he said. "Or try to!"

"I'm not hard to keep up with," she said.

"Except when you're driving!"

"That old Shelton house," Roma said, taking the fresh drink he handed her, "why do you want it? Because it was Roseanne's house?"

"No. I want it because I want to see it stay here in Newfound."

"Did you not know about her boy, either—about Buddy?"

61

"I knew she'd brought him back here, when he was no more than a baby, and left him with her parents. But I never thought I'd be running into him like—like I did today."

"I worry what will become of him," Roma said.

10

Jennings was still sitting on the screened-in porch, talking and drinking with Roma. She had found his battered copy of *How America Came to Cordell County* and was reading aloud from it when Buddy called out from the yard. "Hey, Jennings!"

Drink in hand, he went down the porch steps into the yard. He stood looking at Buddy, then crossed to where Buddy stood kicking the ground with the heel of his shoe. "What say, Henry?"

"I told you, I'm Buddy."

"You're Buddy, but you're a Henry, too. What did you do with those pictures you were carrying?"

Buddy motioned. "Yonder against your shed."

"What can I do for you, Henry?"

"You know, Jennings," Buddy said, "I got to thinking—I need to borrow your pickup."

"What are you talking about, Henry?"

"I aim to live by myself, and there's some stuff down at the Trash & Treasure—I've already been thinking about it."

"I told you, you're a Henry!" Jennings said.

Buddy continued, ignoring Jennings' teasing. "I'm gonna hunt, fish, trap, dig some ginseng. Do jobs for you. Work around. If I could borrow your pickup . . ."

Jennings looked around as the screen door slammed behind Roma, who came down the porch steps and joined them. "I knew I was right when I named you Henry," he said, winking at Roma. "You're a Henry, all right. Gonna drive life into a corner, right, Henry?"

"I keep telling you, I'm Buddy! I wouldn't need that pickup more than about two hours. Trash & Treasure, they stay open till nine tonight."

"If you're not careful, Henry, life's gonna drive *you* into a corner," Jennings said. "Why, you wouldn't last, by yourself, till the snow flies! Your place is with your Grandma and Grandpa and in school."

"Buddy, I wish you'd listen to Jennings," Roma said.

Buddy leaned against Jennings' car there by the maple tree. "No telling how much I can make digging sang. I know what it looks like. I know where to look for it, how to dry it, and all. I helped Grandpa Shelton dig some. People—they've always dug sang here in the mountains. The old pioneers, back in the old days."

"No, they've not always dug it," Jennings said.

"Maybe not always, but a long time," Buddy argued.

"Just how long do you figure, Henry?"

"Four, five hundred years?" Buddy looked up at Jennings.

"Henry," Jennings said gently, "people haven't lived here that long. Indians, yes. But not the rest of us." He looked to Roma for support.

"That's right, Buddy," Roma said. "This place wasn't settled till the late 1700's, early 1800's."

"There's 1847 whittled on Grandpa and Grandma Shelton's house," Buddy volunteered. "On a timber over the door."

"People here didn't know about ginseng till they learned about it from Andre Michaux," Jennings said. He cocked his head. "Or was it Bartram?" He was pretty sure it was Michaux.

"Who's Michaux?" Buddy asked.

"French naturalist," Jennings said.

"I remember," Roma said. "He explored up and down the mountains two hundred years ago, gathered plants."

"See?" Jennings said. "Roma's been to school!"

"I read it, in your book," Roma said.

Jennings sat down beside Roma at the makeshift table under the maple. "If Michaux hadn't told folks there was a market for ginseng, in China, they might not have got word of it for another hundred years! Michaux introduced the mimosa tree into this country, too. Like the one behind your Grandma and Grandpa Shelton's house."

"How'd you know there's a mimosa tree in the backyard down there?" Buddy wanted to know.

"I saw it just this afternoon," Jennings said. "Anyway, I've been over there before."

"When?" Buddy asked.

"Long time ago, when I was half your age and twice your size," Jennings said.

"Back in the old days?"

Jennings grinned. "Yeah, back in the old days."

"Grandma Shelton told me about something that happened back in the old days," Buddy said. "Happened to her Mama, my Great-Grandma Spivey. All these people came from all around one night in the fall, to this one house, for a cornshucking.

Some of the women put their babies in the back room of the house, on a bed. And after the cornshucking, when everybody started heading back home, Great-Grandma Spivey's mama went in the back room and got her baby, and was halfway home, in a wagon, when she went to feed the baby and found out it wasn't her baby she had!"

"You're kidding!" Roma said.

"No," Buddy said. "See, in the dark, she'd picked up the wrong baby!"

"So," Jennings said, nodding. He knew the story in half a dozen versions.

"So they turned the wagon there in the road and started back and met another wagon. It was another woman and her husband. They'd found out they had the wrong baby, too. So they switched babies there in the road and all went home. That was my great-grandma, Grandma Shelton's Mama, that was one of the switched babies. One of the pictures I left down there on your porch, that's her. I figure maybe I could have been switched, and nobody found out about it."

What is this boy up to? Jennings wondered. "You're a mixed-up boy, Henry," he said, "not a mixed-up baby."

"There's this woman over on Lost Creek," Buddy said, "they say she's got what they call the second sight—you know about that?—and she can see through to what's going to happen, see the future. I wonder if she can see backwards, too. If I thought she could, I'd go over there. They say she'll talk to you for ten dollars. Tell you stuff."

The boy was making Jennings uneasy. He glanced at Roma. "Talk to your Grandma and Grandpa Shelton, Henry.—Have they not ever talked to you—about your Mama?"

Buddy shook his head.

66

"Well, what about your Mama?" Jennings asked. "Did she ever talk to you?"

Buddy shook his head again. "I just barely remember her. I just know who she is from her picture."

Jennings studied his near-empty glass. "Well. Anyway. They didn't live back in the old days the way you think, Henry. Didn't just walk around in the woods wearing coonskin caps, barking squirrels with muzzleloaders, wrestling bears . . . ."

"How do you know so much?" Buddy asked.

"I learned it," Jennings snapped. "In school. Do you know that word—school?"

"You don't have to go to school to live in the woods," Buddy said, looking off toward the ridge tops. "And that's where I aim to live."

Jennings downed the rest of his drink and set the glass hard on the table. "I dispute that, Henry. I believe you can live in the woods better if you've been to school. Live in the country better if you've been to town. Now, old Henry Thoreau went to school before he went to the woods."

Still leaning against Jennings' car, Buddy looked around at Jennings. "I believe if I asked you, 'Do you think it'll rain?' you'd work it back around to school!"

"You know why?" Jennings asked. "Because that's where you need to be!"

"Are you all going to argue?" Roma asked.

"We already are arguing," Jennings said. He pushed his empty glass over to her. "Yes, sir, Henry Thoreau went to school before he went to the woods, and when he was living out at the Pond, he went to town about every day."

"I'll go to The Trading Post!" Buddy said.

Jennings thought of The Trading Post—that crossroads

67

store, with its loafers bench and horseshoe pits, and, now that the lake had been created, old barns and outbuildings used for storing power boats. "Not hardly the same, somehow!" he said, glancing at Roma, who got up to replenish their drinks.

Buddy was silent a minute, then said: "Is the key to the pickup in the ashtray, like it usually is?"

"Henry, what do you think you're up to?" Jennings said.

"Well, when I first thought of it," Buddy said, "I was gonna get some stuff from Trash & Treasure and haul it to Grandma and Grandpa's house. But now you're tearing their house down. When you get it put back together, over here somewhere, maybe I can live in it here. Right now, I figure I can live in that old house of yours up the holler there."

"Henry, Henry!" Jennings said. The boy was thinking to live in an old tenant house in the Gudger Hollow.

"Well, nobody's living in it," Buddy said.

"That's because nobody *could* live in it! Why, nobody's lived there since I was a boy."

Roma came out of the house with fresh drinks and sat down with them beside Jennings at the makeshift table.

"I'll be your renter," Buddy said. "And if I can't pay you, I'll work it out."

Jennings reached for his drink. "I've decided I'm not going to let you work for me anymore, Henry. Just now, I decided that."

"How come?"

"If I let you work for me, at piddling jobs, I'll just be helping you stay out of school. Now, your Grandma and Grandpa's house is coming down. It was bound to happen, once they moved out. The Army Corps paid them for their house and land, and . . ."

"Grandpa Shelton never did take that money!" Buddy said. His chin jutted out. "Grandpa never wanted to leave there.

Grandma, neither. It was Hilliard—he sided with the law—against his own Mama and Daddy!"

"The money was put in escrow for them," Jennings said. "All that was in the paper—how it took a court order to get them out down there. That's what got me to thinking about the house." He jerked his head toward Roma. "Roma knows that's so."

"If you won't rent me that house in the Gudger Holler, I'll just go up there and live anyway!"

"Well, go on then! See how long you last!" Jennings said.

"Key in the ashtray?" Buddy asked.

"Yes!" Jennings said, shaking his head, put out by the way the boy had got his way. "Now go on!" He laid his head against Roma's shoulder and said, "This is not a boy—more like an affliction!"

He sat there with Roma watching Buddy back the old red pickup out of the shed and drive off down the road.

"Is it all right for him to drive?" Roma asked.

"No," Jennings said. "But he does have a license."

"Where'd he learn to drive?"

"I guess he was born knowing how," Jennings said.

"You taught him, didn't you?" Roma said. "His Grandpa Shelton didn't have a car."

"No, I didn't teach him. He could drive when he first started coming over here. Said he learned to drive on a log truck . . . somebody he worked for. But I did go into Jewell Hill with him to get his license. Probably shouldn't have. He's a pretty good boy, but . . ."

"And he's Roseanne's boy," Roma said.

Jennings put his hand on Roma's. "I know what you're thinking . . . know there was a lot of talk, and you must have heard it all. But—"

"Let's go somewhere," Roma said.

"Someplace where that boy can't find us!" Jennings said. In the presence of both Roma and Buddy he felt uneasy. And he knew why. Roma kept saying things like, "And he's Roseanne's boy," as if she were explaining something to herself. He wondered just how much talk there had been, years ago, when Roseanne went her way and he went his, when Roseanne brought Buddy back and left him to be raised by her parents. What would Roma have heard back in those days? He'd talk to her about that sometime. But not now.

11

Later that night under a quarter moon he drove alone up on Newfound Hill, to the cemetery, parked near the hickory trees, and walked out among the tombstones of people he had cared most about in the world. Ever. His Grandmother Smith, who sang him old songs in garden patches while they hoed; his Grandmother Wells, with her pretentions to gentility and her classification of people as good livers and the sorry (smiling to himself he remembered the time he'd crept on hands and knees through a back bedroom of the house to get Jeanette's birthday gift for their Grandfather Wells, while his Grandmother Wells gave his sister Jeanette and his brother Eugene a geography lesson in the parlor); his Grandfather Wells, whose left hand had been cut off in a silage cutter when he was a young man; who wore a stocking-like sleeve on the stump where his left hand had been, a brown everyday sleeve, and a blue one to match his Sunday suit; who read Zane Grey novels, newspapers, and commented laconically on any foolishness at the national, state, or local level that came to his attention; his father and his many business ventures; his mother, who was punished unjustly for losing a carpenter's level when she was a little girl, and who waited thirty-five years until a set of steps were torn away revealing the lost level for her vindication.

The quarter moon put him in mind of those nights, when he was twelve and his Grandfather Smith was—what?—seventy, and he'd go foxhunting with the old man. His Grandfather Smith had loved his hounds. Jennings remembered the dog lot: beyond stacked chimneys of stove wood standing yellow in sunlight, drying among craters made by chickens bathing in loose chips—sudden shade. And the dog lot in a clump of pines, an airy bedroom, half a dozen A-frame doghouses gray as hornet nests scattered among the trees. Mornings after a hunt the big-boned Walker foxhounds would be asleep in the houses, curled on straw and burlap, heads lying across their tails. They woke in their own sweet time. Then you'd hear the rub and bump of chains dragged over seasoned boards. And the good sound of dogs lapping water. They'd stretch, shake ragged ears, lick fresh wounds—ripped on brush, briar, and barbed wire—lick private places. They'd walk up and down, their leads running on wires stretched between jackpines.

Jennings remembered walking among the hounds, smelling sheep dip, mange medicine. He remembered their names: Jamup, Honey, Smoky, Luke. A lemon bitch, his grandfather's favorite, named Lady. He'd fondle their ears, their muzzles, shake their proffered paws. He had a word for every droopy face.

Afternoons the hounds would doze, in and out of their houses. An ear would flick a fly away; an old scar would twitch. They'd whine, yelp in their sleep, unraveling the trail a phantom fox laid down in their dreams. By evening, when chickens walked up slanting poles or flew to the lowest limbs of trees to roost, his grandfather's hounds were up and about, pacing the lot, sprinters running in place. They'd wind the evening air, keen for a smell of red, ready for a race.

Back then Jennings thought his grandfather had grown hard of hearing because hair grew from the old man's ears, like mistletoe on an ancient tree. The story was, his grandfather's foxhunting buddies had started telling how one night old man Fred mistook a distant train whistle down by the river for the wailing of his Walker foxhound, Luke. The old man's buddies had liked telling that one so much, he'd stopped hunting with them.

Instead, he'd invite Jennings to go with him, to Grassy, or Horse Knob, although he couldn't hear the chase unless the baying hounds brought the fox close by, or broke out in full clamor on a ridgetop. And sometimes he'd mistake a creaking limb for the high-pitched yap of his lemon bitch, Lady. But ninety percent of foxhunting was getting out of the house, the old man said. So when the hounds ranged far, or trailed down a deep cove between high hills, and the music of the chase became for him what Jennings thought must be like snatches of song on some far-off radio station—when that happened, Jennings would become the old man's ears. Would sit beside him on a moonlit night, or, in cold weather, by a crackling chestnut fire, and tell his grandfather how the hounds were running, whether Jamup and Honey, or Luke and Lady led the chase.

It had been years since he'd sat out on a ridge in moonlight like this. Thirty-five years since he'd become his grandfather's ears. Now, as he walked among the graves, in an old jacket smelling of wood smoke, he thought the old man's feet had become his—patient, steadily climbing.

All those years ago, he thought, it had been a trade: he'd lent the old man his ears, and though he hadn't realized it, the old man had given him eyes—or at least a way of looking at things. And tackling them. A trade.

He considered how his life resembled his grandfather's, and how it differed. For the first seventeen years of his life, Jennings had lived rooted in this one place much as his grandfather had lived all his life. Now he thought of all the places he'd lived since leaving Newfound, and not counting dormitories and temporary stays abroad, he figured he'd lived in more than twenty apartments or houses which, at the time, he considered permanent residences.

He remembered hearing his grandfather speak of a brother, Will, who moved from Newfound when the brothers were in their twenties. For years the old man told of their youthful exploits, but after Will left, they never saw one another, never even heard from one another. Will had moved down into South Carolina, what for Jennings was a day's drive, a two-dollar telephone call, or a postage stamp away.

What Jennings had come to think of as home was a much larger area than what his grandfather had considered home. But not at first. After college he'd come straight back to Cordell County and taught two stormy years in the Cordell County schools, until he was informed his services were no longer required. So he'd gone back to school, in Tennessee. He'd taught then a year at Randolph Macon, a year at Haverford College. But he never felt at home in those places. Home, he came to realize, was a region, an area made up of the mountain backyards of eight or nine states (and all of West Virginia), what the books called southern Appalachia. Home for him was a place where he understood what somebody described as the thousands of feelings and ideas that are tacitly assumed and that constantly glimmer in the background. Or, as somebody else put it, home wasn't where the heart was, but where you understood the S.O.B.s.

But it was more than just understanding other people. It was feeling linked to them. More even than that: I'm not myself, Jennings thought. At least not just myself. I'm mostly other people. For it seemed to him it was his grandfather's hand he held out in night air soft as mole's fur; his grandfather's eyes that saw the quarter moon holding water for September rains.

12

Editor
Cordell County Courier

Dear Sir:

In a recent editorial you expressed concern about Cordell County's loss of skilled and educated young people. Then you suggested taxing the incomes of people who had been educated in the county, but who had gone elsewhere to earn a living. The tax ought to be levied on the incomes of teachers, doctors, lawyers, and skilled workers for the first twenty years of their employment outside the county.

A unique proposal, certainly. No. More nearly harebrained. Feudal. Does a county own a person because he or she is accidentally born there?

I would like to point out the obvious: Cordell County hasn't educated a single teacher, doctor, or lawyer. The high school emphasizes vocational training, and even so, seventy-five percent of its graduates have to go out of the county to find jobs. Most of those who have gone on to college or university elsewhere (and I number myself among these) couldn't hope to return to Cordell County, because opportunities for professionals and highly-skilled workers are strictly limited here.

This is an old problem, which, I suspect, has no satisfactory solution. People have been drawn away from the place of their birth since Catullus went up to Rome, since German boys joined the Roman legions as mercenaries. And surely for centuries before that. If the writer of Genesis had been a sociologist, he would have noted that there were unemployed people living down in the boondocks who got word there was work up at the Tower of Babel, and so they struck out, men with wives and children, single mothers with three kids, unattached males, and lived in a trailer-jungle near the construction site. Living in London in the late 19th century, Arnold Bennett, the novelist, commented that he knew hardly any native Londoners. Almost everyone he knew had, like himself, come from the provinces.

People leave home. I did. Then at some point, for economic, professional, political, or even spiritual reasons, they discover they can never return. Certainly since Thomas Wolfe wrote his last novel it has been axiomatic that you can't go home again.

I don't believe it. Obviously, many people all over the country do leave home, are educated, and then return permanently to live just half a mile down the road from Mama and Papa. They return as teachers, doctors, administrators, social workers. They enter family businesses, the law firm with their father and three brothers. I believe you can go home again, even in Appalachian Cordell County.

I've paid taxes in other places for a lot of years, and will be happy to pay taxes in Cordell County now that I'm back here. But I hope I won't be billed for back taxes on all the years I've been gone!

Robert Jennings Wells
Newfound

13

They drove. She'd persuaded him to have a tape deck installed in his Skyhawk—wouldn't ride in his car until he got the tape deck. She'd even picked it out, made an appointment at a garage, and went there with him one evening and supervised the mechanic, whom she knew as Willis. She gave Jennings a special cassette, one she had put together of her favorites—Old Regular Baptist hymns alternating with raucous rockabilly and bluegrass. He'd heard a lot of them, years ago, could still sing along on some of them. All that seemed so long ago to him now. Still, the songs bristled with connotations for him, riveted his attention sometimes, chilled him with their directness and simplicity. He found himself playing a Stanley Brothers version of "Spare Me Over Another Year."

"If that don't bring your heart home, I don't know what will," he said.

"What I figured," Roma said. She sat in the Skyhawk staring

straight ahead, her head bobbing gently to the rhythm of the music.

They drove. Had supper at a truck stop out by the interstate. Then drove again, listening to country music on the radio. Jennings drove to the heads of creeks he hadn't been on in twenty years. No, thirty. And ended up on Spring Creek, at the site of the old Rocky Top Festival. Parked, like teenagers. Got out and walked the creek bank by moonlight, came back to the car covered in sticktights, laughing, then sat talking quietly—of bad times, losses, broken marriages.

"Are you married—still?" Roma wanted to know. No. He'd been divorced now a couple of years. He told Roma about his marriage to a divorcee with a daughter and two half-grown sons. Hadn't worked out, neither with her nor with her boys. He'd been stupid to think her sons would share his enthusiasms. He'd tried to introduce them to woods, fields, waters, to rods and reels, guns, waders, depth finders, trolling motors. There would be nights, he'd thought, when hissing lanterns, hung out of the boat, lit still green water back up under willows. A rod tip would twitch, there'd be a grunt, a scramble for the rod as it bent double, throbbing. Later, maybe, nights in an old house, or a tent, a belt of Jim Beam's bourbon, coffee, cigarettes. Tall tales, outrageous lies, stories of famous snipe hunts, run-ins with the legendary wampus cat. Poontang. And pickup trucks. The boys would learn to drive a straight-shift on a red clay wagon road, where grass grew high between the ruts, in sight of gray tobacco barns.

"You just wanted to make good old boys out of them," Roma said.

"I sent that story out to them," he said. "It came back: 'Sorry, this doesn't meet our present needs.'"

80

No, those boys had been buying a different kind of fiction. Smoked funny cigarettes. Styled their hair with a hot comb, noticed the thickness of carpeting, wanted to look like people in advertisements. Lived in a halfway house of pounding music that sounded like a crew installing dry wall. Shit. Now he could see there was no reason why they should be what he wanted them to be, and every reason for them not to be. At the time though, he'd leaned pretty hard on them. And made things worse. One threw a chair at him. The other slashed his photo. Together they stole the car! He was a failure with the daughter too. "I know a rejection when I've been slipped one," Jennings told Roma. "I filed that story away."

Still, he took it out again from time to time, ran it through his mind again. It was still a good story. Dammit.

Jennings recalled his father, told how his mother, after years of trying, had finally got his father to quit drinking—though he wasn't much of a drinker—even persuaded him, there toward the end, to join the church. Then his father had come home one night—that's how his mother later told it—stood in the doorway, and said: "What difference does it make?" He'd had a few drinks. Despite the lapse, the minister who preached his funeral said Jennings' father died in the fold, the Lord having "found him in a field." Jennings wasn't so sure the "found me in a field" line wasn't the minister's invention, spun out of the Twenty-third Psalm. Nice, though. "Found me in a field." He sat there with Roma listening to the Stanley Brothers tape. "Well, what is this that I can't see / With ice-cold hands taking hold of me?"

He remembered his father's long dying. He and his mother had understood, finally, why his father had the tops of the white pines cut out—those beautiful pines that grew back of the house and all along both sides of the drive. And why his father had argued with the man he'd hired to do it, claiming the job hadn't been done to suit him.

But Jennings and his mother certainly hadn't understood at the time. Whatever had possessed his father, Jennings wondered when his mother told him about it in a letter, to want the tops cut out of those lovely trees, a good third of every tree removed, so that they stood amputated, ugly? What kind of damned fool notion! But he was always getting some fool notion nobody else saw the sense of—like the time he thought he'd get rich making cement blocks; or the time he took up raising goats! So, they'd figured he was just being the way he'd always been, only a little more so. Later they'd understood that when he had the trees topped he was already making his last stand.

He never said why he had the white pines mutilated, but it must have been because he thought they were keeping air away from the house. For not long after that he started buying fans— window fans, floor fans, ceiling fans—to increase the circulation of air inside the house. After he had the trees topped, he wanted doors left open, so air could freely circulate. But when he got all the fans, and then the air conditioner, he wanted doors kept closed. He had all the windows sealed, the shades and curtains drawn in the room where he'd had the window air conditioning unit placed.

If, a short time earlier, he'd wanted all outdoors inside, now he barricaded himself against the outdoors, against the muggy summer, pollen, against whatever it was; and from the cool darkness of their bedroom, he'd railed at Jennings' mother when she opened a door. For now he seemed to have seen it— this thing he had made a stand against—and it wasn't in the house, it was outside.

But what had come next from outside was a tank of oxygen.

One night when he wanted more than it was gauged to give, he took a pocketknife and tinkered with the gauge. Later they'd been told it was a wonder he hadn't blown the whole house up. It simply wouldn't do to go to sleep and leave him free to tinker with the oxygen supply.

Then came nurses, a different one for every eight-hour shift. Sitting up, or lying in bed, he'd stare at a lamp, or a picture on the wall, and decide it wasn't just the way it should be, and have the nurse move it. A little later he'd want it moved again. "But we just moved that lamp," the nurse would say. He didn't give a damn. She could move it again.

He'd had a habit, as long as Jennings could remember, of taking something you said and repeating it back to you with a twist, sometimes amusingly garbled. (He was not hard of hearing.) This little perversity he carried to his last stand. Jennings had driven the three hundred and fifty miles back home one night, and slipped in quietly at four a.m. He eased down on the sofa and lay in the quiet house listening to the hissing of the oxygen dispenser in his father's room. Then he slept. And woke when the nurses changed shifts at seven. He heard the day nurse, fresh and cheerful, say, "Did you know your son came home last night?"

"My money?" he'd heard his father say—and recognized the old conversational gambit. "What about my money?"

"No, your son."

"Yeah."

"He came home last night."

"Yeah."

His oxygen supply had a long transparent hose that permitted him to come from his room to the breakfast table. He sat there, talked a little. His voice was strong but his eyes were almost closed. "Dad, this is Jennings," he said. "I drove in last night."

His father didn't acknowledge him in any way. Later his father said, "I'm through talking now," and told the nurse he wanted up. Jennings helped him to his feet, and, with the help of the day nurse, one of them on either side, making sure the oxygen line didn't get caught or twisted, they walked him back to his room and helped him into bed.

Jennings felt oddly relieved that his father no longer seemed to know him, and then ashamed for feeling relieved.

He remembered his father as he'd been before he'd had the trees topped, before the fans,—how, on the rare occasions, usually Christmas, when Jeanette would be home with her children, like an old dog annoyed by playful pups, he'd mark his place in his history of World War II, leave the table of grandchildren and their loud games, and come into the living room to find another grandchild in his easy chair; how he'd grin, and shake his head, pleased to be so put upon, and coax the grandchild from his chair, or compromise, and let the child sit in his lap.

That sort of scene, that time, was gone forever now. And it was harder and harder for him to come back from that place he'd turn his head to. He even looked different now—his face puffy, his hands and arms covered with purple needle splotches. And then he worsened in that heat wave Jennings seemed to have brought with him from Virginia. He gulped for air until his stomach was inflated. Sitting on the gurney as he was carried out of the house, into the ambulance they'd called, his face puffed, his belly round and tight, he looked like a little Buddha, not at all like Jennings' father.

When he could no longer breathe deeply enough, even with the aid of oxygen, a respirator forced him to inhale. The machine forced oxygen and medication in . . . and in . . . and in; then the exhalation came, hideously, on its own. When this procedure was initiated, and he lay propped, a mask taped over his face, he must have felt his breath had already been taken from him, for it was no longer his own breathing.

He must have learned, during this time, that breath was not in the expanding and contracting, the inhaling and exhaling. Breath was somewhere else. Where? He would find it.

For two days and nights he looked for it. For two days and nights he never closed his eyes. He stared, alert, as if he thought death might come through the door, and if death entered, he would see death before death caught sight of him. Maybe he thought he was still at home, where he seemed first to have the notion that death was outside the house, and if he could keep the doors closed and the windows sealed . . . .

But now he was the house, and death had already entered, was sitting quietly, holding something in its hand. And now death stirred, and moved about the house, closing doors, switching off lights. In the dark death had held out a hand— and given his father a stone to breathe.

Trying to reach his father, toward the end, had been like trying to lift a reflection off a pool. His father's mind had shattered into a Guernica of horses' heads, barns, bear hunts. For a long time Jennings had believed his father was still there between the sheets. Finally, he realized that, like the boy who stuffs his pajamas with old shirts and dirty underwear, and slips out the window in the dark, his father had left and now was hurrying to catch up with his runaway mind.

Maybe he went looking for his lost tools, Jennings thought, at the time.

Still he reached for his father sometimes, the way he patted himself over the heart, feeling for a pair of mislaid reading glasses. Or sometimes, especially now that he was back home, he'd come on his father unexpectedly, as if his father were the missing lock pliers, discovered in a drawer while he was looking for duct tape.

He could carry his father's memory with him, the way he carried his father's pocket knife in an old army field jacket.

When he held it to his ear, he could hear his father's watch still ticking.

He could drive his father's old pickup about the place. When he forded Newfound Creek in the old truck, it sometimes died.

But the truck always lived again.

"Excuse me?" Roma said.

Jennings realized he'd been sitting there a long time listening to the Stanley Brothers and remembering his father, and hadn't spoken a word to Roma.

She knew he liked some of the old songs but she still wasn't sure he liked the country music she played on the radio. Even in the old Rocky Top Festival, years ago, all he'd ever sung with Roseanne Shelton was old-timey ballads. Jennings had played a guitar then, she remembered. Did he ever play now?

He hadn't played in years. All that was another country, it seemed to him now.

Roma told about her first date. When she was fourteen, this boy, John L. Freeman, asked her to be his date for a dance at the school. She looked forward to that dance for days. She and her mother made a green velvet dress with a big bow, and when she walked in to the dance that night (John L. wasn't supposed to pick her up, just be her date at the dance)—when she walked in, everybody else had on jeans—and there she stood in a green velvet dress with a big bow.

That was only the first of several miscalculations she'd made. Her first marriage, for instance. Pipes froze in the trailer they first lived in, and her husband, Roger Devasher, wouldn't get them fixed. She had no water for a week, and her with Karen, only about two months old then. Karen was almost eighteen now and had lived with her grandmother after Roma had gone to school; Karen hardly seemed like her daughter now. Water had been so precious during that cold time, if something stuck in a pot or pan when she tried to cook, she threw the pan away rather than waste water washing it! Had to go to her mother's to bathe—herself and the baby! Roma covered her face with both hands and shook her head remembering. And recalled her second husband.

Who was that? Jennings wanted to know.

It slipped her mind! No, she just couldn't bring herself to call his name. Anyway, he wasn't around Newfound any longer. Roger Devasher wasn't, either. But she'd done everything but wear candy pants for Whatshisname, that sonofabitch. And he'd treated her like a baloney string! Her first marriage broke up because Roger Devasher was no-count. After her second marriage failed—and it hadn't lasted six months—she began to think there was something wrong with *her*. She bent her head low till her hair fell over her face.

Was she asking him for an opinion? Jennings wondered.

Maybe.

Well, he didn't think there was anything wrong with her.

He looked over at her. Her face could be so bright when she smiled. Now, in the dim light inside the car with the window rolled down so he could hear Spring Creek running, by the old pavilion where the Rocky Top Festival had been held years ago, Roma's face looked to Jennings like a Walker Evans photo of a mountaineer or mill worker. She'd had her share of troubles, he said, but . . . .

She thought maybe she was trouble.

No. He shook his head.

He'd have to admit, though, *something* was wrong. Maybe she was just stupid. After all, anybody would have to be pretty dumb to drive their ducks to a poor pond *twice*.

He smiled. No, she'd been young, not dumb. If she'd stayed with either one of her husbands, it seemed to him, *that* would have been dumb. She'd been treated bad.

Yeah. Rode hard and put up wet! But they'd always said this place was hard on women and mules.

It appeared to Jennings, that in spite of everything, she'd done well for herself. Got out of all that, gone to school, got a job, had her own place.

Roma looked out at the old pavilion. Jennings wouldn't have come up there—to Rocky Top—if she hadn't suggested it, would he?

Eventually, maybe.

Rocky Top was a lot of memories for him, wasn't it?

Yeah. Everything was coming back fast. The old Shelton house. Roseanne's boy. Roma.

Roma wondered: Roseanne—did she ever . . . ? Roma thought maybe Jennings heard from Roseanne sometimes.

No. He hadn't heard from her in years. Wouldn't know where she was.

Had she said the wrong thing, bringing up Roseanne?

No, it was all right. That was all over, years ago.

She knew she took up his time, pulled him away from his work. But then, she meant to! She was warning him, she was trouble!

Maybe she was trouble, and maybe she was warning him. But Jennings had already begun to suspect that Roma was only speeding up something that was already happening to him.

Even before he'd decided to come back to Newfound, he'd been working his way back home. During his father's illness, he'd been home several times. And earlier this year, after his mother's death, he'd come back—done some fixing up around the house, repaired a barn roof. Working up a sweat there on top of the barn, he'd first thought about taking a leave and coming back home to work. Now, a few months later, here he sat, by the old Rocky Top pavilion with Roma Jean Livesay. He guessed Roma thought he'd come home a few days before she drove up, that afternoon, in her Mercury. Maybe so, but he'd started home, he realized, that day back in the spring when he was on the barn roof repairing it.

He figured it must be easier to go home in other parts of the country. But he wasn't sure about that. But here in Appalachia, unless you belonged to a tiny elite, going home could be difficult. Sometimes impossible. If you were born in a coal camp, your home literally might not be there any longer. He remembered a news story about the actress Patricia Neal who returned once to Knoxville for a reunion of her high school class. But she couldn't return to Packard, Kentucky, where she was born. The town ceased to exist when the mine was closed. Billy Edd Wheeler, the song writer, couldn't go home to Highcoal, West Virginia. The people, the houses, post office—they were all gone. Where Wheeler went to school, there was nothing but squirrels, birds, and the sound of the creek running.

If you were born in a place like Packard or Highcoal, your family might be living in Cincinnati now, or Toledo, or Cleveland, or Detroit. Or your family might be marginal farmers still living on the land but actually earning a living from some 40-hour-a-week job at a paper mill, or a factory thirty-five miles away. If you were educated or trained for a particular skill or

89

profession, there was less likelihood you'd be able to return to the place where you were born. Unless you had put in the years somewhere else and could retire, like Jennings.

Most people, Jennings knew, just assumed they wouldn't ever go home again. They didn't agonize over it.

Did Roma think he was agonizing?

No. She thought she understood how he felt. She was glad she'd been able to come back after going away to school.

Did Roma think any American could write about the realization of not being able to go home with as much feeling as Wolfe did in 1940?

Roma wasn't sure. She suspected, though, that if you said, "You can't go to the mall again," there'd be a great outcry.

Jennings grinned. If Wolfe were in his late thirties and writing today, he doubted whether going home would be an issue for Wolfe. In Wolfe's last book, George Webber sought the help of America's "little people," realizing that greed and selfishness, purporting to be the friends of mankind, were keeping America from finding herself. More than thirty years later another George (McGovern) called, "Come home, America," but the Winnebago motor homes all headed for the territory!

Roma remembered that.

The only other writer Jennings knew who had written about leaving home and being unable to return, who even remotely approached Wolfe, was Willie Morris. In a book called *North Toward Home* Morris had written about how he felt both alienated from the South and yet drawn to it. But the tension was slacker than in Wolfe or Faulkner.

Roma wanted to know if Jennings was talking to her or just to himself.

Both, maybe.

As far as she was concerned, he was home. What she thought

he ought to do was to get out more, and not just sit humped up over a typewriter day after day. She thought maybe she'd put him into circulation!

He had no idea what she had in mind, but he knew he would find out.

14

At first Jennings had pretended Roma was an intrusion, dropping by the way she did, arriving always to the sound of country music. But when she didn't come by one afternoon, he'd missed her, and kept glancing at his watch. Finally he drove over to her house and found a pickup parked there. The next day he'd asked her who had been at her house. Somebody named Darrell; he came by sometimes. Didn't she know how to get rid of him? he'd asked. She didn't want to get rid of him, she'd said. And he realized he was jealous.

Since Roma had driven into his life, trailing country music, he'd had to remind himself who he was and what he'd come home to do. Because, dammit, he wasn't getting any work done! Or very little. He had half a dozen projects in various stages of completion—or better, incompletion. There were those translations of work by an Austrian poet. He'd tried working at them but, to tell the truth, the Austrian's poems paled beside Roma's vivid presence. He'd brought along the start of a longish essay tentatively called "Wit on the Stairs," and hadn't been able to move it forward, either. After a few pages of dry, cerebral stuff he'd found himself thinking of Roma, or, rather, of the two Romas—the little girl there on the porch steps of the Livesay house, years ago, and this disturbingly vivid woman he was getting to know. The two images were always with him now, like two photographs above his worktable.

He'd tried to work on his own poems, too, and found he'd lost all interest in them. Instead, he started a poem about Roma, and girls he recollected from his adolescence.

> Those girls: gadgets with secret compartments,
> drawers, little knobs. Novelties. . . .

Where to go with it from there? He knew he was resisting going anywhere with it, knew he should lay aside the translations, the essay, his poems, and get on with the book about New-found, and all the change that had come to this place and the surrounding region. That was the book he'd really come back to work on. And, after all, he'd become something of a spokes-man for the region, its problems and potential. He'd sit, trying to work, and a long time later realize he'd been sitting at his worktable remembering the delightful rise and fall of Roma's voice, having an imaginary conversation with her, just to hear her speak. He'd be thinking about how she was always turning to him with something unexpectedly vulgar—and wondering how she would react if he said to her, apropos of nothing, "I saw your twat once."

She was funny. And fun to be with. But Roma could humble him, too. Show him his faults. For one thing, she wasn't im-pressed with his reputation. Interested, but not necessarily im-pressed. He cringed inwardly when he thought about how she had kept up with him over the years, hearing about him through his mother, or cousins, and he hadn't even known until recently that she had gone to college, too, the only one of the Livesay children to do so. He hadn't even known who she was when she drove up that afternoon—thought she was some crazy!

Funny, and fun. Yes. But sometimes she got so low, despite his efforts to make her laugh. So down on herself. Just the other day she talked a long time about her brother Craig, who'd been killed in Vietnam and was buried in the Newfound Cemetery. Jennings remembered the boy, a couple of years older than Roma, both of them younger than their brother Clyde, the Livesay boy he hunted with. Sitting on the floor remembering her brother Craig, her feet drawn up underneath her, Roma had looked up at Jennings, then away. He turned her chin back toward him with his forefinger and looked down into the saddest eyes he'd ever seen. Tears welled in her eyes. She'd looked haunted, lost. Craig had been killed in 1967, but the grief that had broken from Roma that evening might have come at the first news of his death. When Craig died, she said, it was like . . . . She bent her left hand back with her right and showed him only her wrist. "Like I lost a hand. And it's never changed. Never will." Jennings remembered the time he'd seen Mrs. Livesay switch one of the boys—maybe it had been Craig—and all the other Livesay children protested and cried with him, as if they were not different kids but all one body.

Roma had drunk too much that evening and gone to sleep at Jennings' house. He read and wrote. When he got up to get coffee and passed the half-open door of the bedroom, he'd seen her lying there—so unbelievably there—naked, on her stomach, her hard buttocks lifting like a wave. Her underwear lay puddled on the floor where she had stepped out of them, her red dress a flame licking across the foot of the bed. Jennings had felt like a spectator at a fire.

She showed him his contradictions. She pointed out how, in books and articles he'd written he had praised the rooted, rural life, yet he'd flitted around, in universities, in Europe, and knew his people more as an idea than as individuals. For instance, he hadn't been to see Edna Rae, once his favorite cousin, in more than fifteen years.

Roma had Edna Rae in mind, he discovered, when she'd said she was going to put Jennings into circulation. She was taking him on as a case, like one of the people assigned to her in Cordell County's Social Services office, where she worked. So on Sunday she drove him up the Green Valley road to see his cousin Edna Rae. When they came in under the big catalpa tree where Edna Rae sat beside a basket of late tomatoes from her garden, Roma said: "Look what I brought you! I reckon he'd sit over there on Newfound, humped up over books and papers, and never get out and about, even to see his own people, if somebody didn't drag him out!"

Edna Rae got up and came to him, smiling her broad smile. "Well, law, law!" And she hugged him. Over the years Jennings had lost touch with Edna Rae. He knew only that her life had been saddened by the death of a son in an auto accident, and the ordeal of her alcoholic husband, Earl. There were two daughters, somewhere. He couldn't remember their names. "I wrote Gerald a letter not long ago," he told Edna Rae, "but I didn't know where to send it."

Another evening Roma circulated him in a pool hall, where he quickly saw she was able to take care of herself. While she bent forward to break, a truck driver walked by and patted her bottom. Without looking up, Roma said: "Do that again, James Ray Pressley, and these ain't the only balls I'll break. You hear?"

Most of the men in the pool hall were in their twenties and thirties and had grown up since Jennings left. If he'd ever seen any of them, they'd have been kids when he left. Some surely hadn't even been born. He didn't trust himself even to spot family resemblances in that crowd of beards and hair curling from beneath feed store hats, like the roofs of pago-. das. But Roma knew them. She'd ask: "Did you ever get your hay in, W. J.?" Or: "How's your Mama, Glen?"—"Some better. Mama got this bunch of papers in the mail, insurance, I reckon. Wished you'd come over and help her figure out what to do, Roma. I can't never tell her."—"I will," Roma said.

She reminded him that before he left Newfound he'd hunted and fished a lot. She borrowed somebody's runabout and they went out on Big Ivy Lake on a warm September evening. He re-discovered an old love—water. Actually, a twin love—of women and water. For they merged in his mind. How many times had he driven to road's end, shouldered a load, and back-packed in to a stretch of sweet-talking water? Or, wet, shivering in coming cold, crashed through a willow thicket in last light, scrambled breathless and betrayed up the rocky bank of water's broken promises. Water was a woman, a woman water. And always, women and water drew him back, and he'd stand in a deep run below loud falls, and feel water flowing around him, an embrace of murmuring thighs. He'd tickled for trout between a woman's thighs, and thought: trout in a creel lined with minty pennyroyal smelled like a spring-fed woman. He'd studied water under willows and caught the dimpling swirl a feeding trout made on the water, like the smile that starts in a woman's eyes. He'd lain spent by a willowy woman slender and springy as a rod tip. A fly rod was such a woman. And Roma, there in the runabout with him, was such a fly rod of a woman. He'd never held her though.

He cut back on the throttle of the borrowed runabout that night, then shut it off completely and let the boat drift silently on the moonlit lake.

By God, geography still existed, despite what Alvin Toffler had maintained in *Future Shock*. Maybe geography wasn't as important as it once was. Lots of people found community nowadays over great distances through electronic bulletin boards! And there were pervasive pressures to remain relatively rootless. There were the rewards of money, prestige, and success for pursuing nomadic existences, for the ability to pull up, take leave overnight, plug in quickly to new situations and size them up swiftly. People were rewarded for the exploitative grasp of new circumstances, the almost predatory reading of people and places. The kind of knowledge that was valued was utilitarian, and, being that, disposable. People had to be able to retool. There wasn't much demand for the kind of knowledge that came of living a long time in one place, knowledge gained slowly with the turning of the seasons, in daily contact with neighbors. (Well, occasionally there was a demand: Hilliard had wanted him to go to work for him, cutting deals with Cordell County property owners, because Jennings knew the place, how people thought.) But for the most part, as a country storekeeper would put it, there weren't many calls for that kind of knowledge.

But people needed to go home, no matter where home was,

and even if only briefly, temporarily. There was something spiritual about it. It was a confrontation with the self, an encounter with everything you were the upshot of . . . .

He hadn't said anything for a long time. Roma wanted to know what he was thinking about.

"This place," he said. "I was remembering how the road ran through here before the lake covered it." And he had been remembering that, too. But anything he might say was a half-truth. The rest flowed on, an underground river.

He sat there, so calm outwardly, but actually amazed at himself, at how he'd got mixed up with this girl—this woman, her head full of country and gospel songs. *Gospel music!* He'd once published a list of things the world could do without, and high on the list had been *gospel music*. Now some of the old songs pulled powerfully at him.

Roma thought maybe he wasn't enjoying himself. She thought maybe he was thinking she was pulling him away from his work.

No, no. He'd just been thinking. About a lot of things. About coming home.

"You're writing," Roma said. "I've figured that out about you. When you get that look, you're writing something in your head."

Roma was right. He was thinking that because people had become such confirmed transients, it was even more important to be able to go home. It mattered to be able to affirm origins, a place, a people, a way of life, a set of relationships. Not to acknowledge those things freely was to lose a part of one's self. Otherwise, we did massive damage to our notion of who we were; we confused ourselves with our many roles. We got lost in the American Fun House and wandered about, seeing distorted images of ourselves. If we walked about in that Fun House long enough, we got accustomed to grotesque images of ourselves: a huge elongated trunk, a bulging wrap-around brow moving on stumpy legs, our belts just above our shoe tops, our chins in our laps, our hands growing right out of our shoulders, no wrists, arms, or elbows in between.

And what was the result? Sickness, despair, alienation. We became what somebody called "genuine fakes." Weird. Grotesque. Spiritual disaster areas. The sort of people who got together, men in one room, women in another, and had separate conversations about the relative merits of kitchen appliances and rider lawn mowers, the talk sounding like simultaneous editorial meetings at *Consumer Reports*. He'd been there.

And now he was back in Newfound. And if being back was different from what he'd thought it, that was because being here was better than he'd imagined. Roma made it better. Even the boy, Buddy, who was living up there in the old house in Gudger Holler now. (He'd been trying not to think about that!) Dismantling the old Shelton house was still unsettling, though; he wondered whether he was really saving it, or, as Buddy had accused him, just tearing it down. He didn't know.

Roma said she knew she pulled him away from his work, held him back. But she didn't care!

No, no, Jennings said, shaking his head. And he tried to explain something to her, something that was happening to him. He couldn't name it. He could only say what it was like. He remembered reading somewhere about how the water of a lake separated out into layers of varying temperatures during the summer. Then in the fall, when the top layer cooled, the lake turned over: the top layer sank to the bottom, the bottom layer rose to the top. He was a lake turning over. All he had been most recently was sinking. All that was subdued in him, his past in this place, was rising to the surface.

No, Roma wasn't holding him back, he told her. She was speeding up something. He was a lake turning over, and she was speeding that up.

"Good!" she said.

They drifted a long time on the lake talking quietly until it was late.

Roma said, "When you get a little tired, you start to sound like I remember, like you talked before you ever left home."

"How can you remember anything about me? You were a little kid then."

"Sometimes I forget what I went to the store for," Roma said. "But I remember everything about you."

He was shamed by how much she remembered about him. He told her he was going to make it up to her, and become the Official Historian of Roma Jean Livesay. She smiled approval of his allusion to a song by the Statler Brothers. But it was true, he was filling in the long blank between the suntanned, black-haired girl on the porch, looking up at him, years ago, and this unsettling woman he was spending more and more time with.

A deep well of a woman, he thought again and again. Deep and clear and fresh and ever-replenishing.

Well, if he was going to become her official historian, she was going to educate him about country music. He was so ignorant, she was embarrassed for him! For one thing, Edna Rae was wanting to go to a Conway Twitty concert. Jennings could take them.

A Conway what? Jennings wanted to know.

15

Buddy came over and talked Jennings into going fishing. The boy never missed an afternoon now. He knew when Jennings usually stopped working, and he'd come up the long drive between the big white pines, and sit on the steps, tapping nervously with a stick, or whittling on a stick with a pocket knife, like an old man, trying all the while to interest Jennings in driving somewhere. And in getting Jennings to let him do the driving. This time they were fishing a farm pond on Sugar Creek.

You couldn't just go fish in somebody's pond without first asking permission, Jennings had objected. Whose pond was it, anyway?

The pond was on old man Jess Teague's place, Buddy said. But Jess Teague had died a long time ago, and nobody lived there now.

When had Jess Teague died? Jennings wondered. He remembered how his mother always clipped obituaries out of the *Cordell County Courier* and saved them until he came home.

He'd ask, since she never dated the clippings, when someone had died, and his mother would begin an endless speculation: now, was it before the bridge washed out? Or after the big snow? As if that dated the clipping for him.

Somebody ran cattle on the Jess Teague place now, Buddy said, and somebody else raised burley tobacco there. But it was all right to fish in the pond.

Jennings smiled to himself, remembering that it was Jess Teague's tom turkey he'd run over, when he was about Buddy's age. And his father had paid Jess fifteen dollars for the turkey. There hadn't been a pond on Jess Teague's place back then.

But there was now, and it looked as if it had been there a long time. An acre and a half, maybe, ringed by briers, tall weeds, and willows. Jennings stood rigging a spinning rod and looking around. Day after dry warm broomsage day for a week now in September when he was out riding around with Buddy he had watched light grow golden over fields. Sometimes the light hung in coppery dust clouds behind green and yellow John Deere combines harvesting soybeans in the bottoms, or tractors plowing the already harvested fields.

Here the light was lemony where willows ringed the some-what shrunken pond, like a crowd at a public sale where the sun auctioned the water off. The air stood between earth and sky like a dry sauterne. Gray barns in the distance, seen as if through the curve of a bottle, rocked gently in the standing light, like warped, weathered boats.

"Plastic worm's what you want to use here," Buddy said, and tossed him one.

"I've fished a little in my time," Jennings said. "But I've not ever used one of these things."

"Not ever used a plastic worm? You don't know what's good then. Guess I'll have to teach you."

Plastic worms. Dear God. He turned the lure between his fingers and thought again of those bleak winters and the coming of spring when they waited for the woods to come alive again, for the arrival of the redhorse in the creeks.

Those boys he ran with, his cousin Gerald, and Clyde Livesay, the Cox boys, Riley and Columbus, Weaver and Everett Sams, Ernest and Jess Barnes, Kermit Worley—there always came a time for them, toward the end of winter, when they lost their faith in woods and waters, and disbelief lay in their hearts like old snow on shaded slopes. Their lives would stand as empty as grey tobacco barns, tin roofs the grey of winter sky, that held nothing but the sharp fragrance of last year's burley. Empty and gray as last year's wasp and hornet nests. Barren as a tree in a pasture corner when a flock of crows flew from it like black leaves blown and left it standing naked.

The woods stood open then, still and motionless, and seemed to hold no secrets, while the distant ridges stood hard as iron. They'd walked the woods all day during such times, always hoping the brown leaves at their feet would thunder up, transformed into pheasants. Waiting for the miracle. It would not come.

Their traps would go undisturbed for days. The slides and trails, tunnels and beds of muskrats would have grown faint, the tracks of mink a month old now in frozen mud. And though sycamores along the creek stood white as skeletons, they'd keep returning, breaking ice at the creek's edge, hoping for the miracle. At night they'd stand in the desolate woods, woods so open they could hear, half a mile away, their hounds working in the leaves. Waiting for the hounds to strike a trail. It would not come.

And so they'd stop believing in the woods. They'd lose their faith in water. Like old men telling stories of their youth, they'd remember the past autumn, when the hollows were filled with the baying of their hounds; when their traps took mink and muskrat; when the ground would come alive under their feet and fly up into their gun sights.—But that was so far past now, they couldn't be sure it all hadn't been a dream. They'd doubt their own memories sometimes, unsure that any of it had happened.

He remembered walking home from some doomed hunt, in a day-long drizzle out of a slate sky, his thoughts working shifts, bent and cramped in a day that had become as close as a mine shaft. Remembered how on such days, drizzle hanging beaded on his hat brim, his mood would have grown damp and heavy as his old hunting coat, his spirit low and dingy like the creek turning between white-barked sycamores that lined the bank.

Then something *would* occur to make them believers once again. Some evening in early March, after the wind lay, they'd come together, maybe, on a ridge to burn a tobacco bed—twenty men and boys and maybe as many hounds. A clearing would have been cut there on the ridge, logs and stumps and brush piled ten feet high and a hundred feet long or longer. They'd rake the ground leaf-free around the bed, light the fire, and stand watching it brighten the surrounding woods. Shadows of great flames would leap toward the woods like darting animals; smoke would roll like a lumbering bear.

At first it would be hard to believe again. After all, the woods had been empty for so long now. Not even when a stump or half a log fell through the stack of burning brush and sparks flew up like a covey of quail and the big fire popped and cracked like their guns firing last fall, even then it was hard to believe the woods were full of anything but shadows. So they'd sit or stand watching the fire, tell tales, maybe roast potatoes in the coals, or spit ham on green sticks over the fire.

Then, when they least expected, it would happen. When no one was even thinking about it any longer, because they were hunted out, talked out, and far down in the hole of winter—just then it might happen. One of the dogs, further up the ridge, would strike a trail, and give mouth: Ooo-ooh! The bark would come urgent as a tapping on a line held between the fingers. And suddenly they'd all be on their feet, listening. While they stood in the clearing, their faces lit by the fire of the burning tobacco bed, one baying hound would bring the woods alive, and they'd all believe again.

Someone would whistle. Someone would call the hound by name. A second hound would join the first, giving mouth. Maybe a couple of dogs that had been curled up near the fire would slip through whining, and hit the dry leaves in a lope, out beyond the fire. Soon the hounds would be a pack, their baying lighting up the woods like their fire. And they'd leave the fire to follow the hounds, their blood aroused, their noses tingling with all the possibilities of wood smoke and awakening earth. Hurrying after the hounds, suddenly believers again, faith in the woods restored by a wildness that entered them in the music of baying hounds.

Jennings threaded a purple worm on his hook, cast out, reeled back. He watched the purple worm come snaking back and saw that the point of the hook had grown a beard of green algae.

"We may need weedless hooks," Buddy said.

Here he was fishing an algae-choked farm pond in the fall, a pond that hadn't even been here when he was growing up. But he remembered so well this place in early spring, when the woods and waters came alive again, and miracles lurked, waiting to be flushed out. Tin-roofed barns gleamed in the sun.

Tobacco beds covered with white canvas bloomed in clearings on ridges, like dogwood blossoms that would come later. Wind that roared in treetops on the slopes turned green and warm over broomsage seas, leaving shadows in the rolling troughs. Then miracles could happen again.

He remembered how, as the sun stayed a little longer each day in March, you'd see small children playing in front of houses, like foxes before their dens. Old men at the crossroads stores sat in the sun. Their hands stirred, eager to plow newground. Shadows of wind-tossed limbs danced against blood-red banks of clay, on gravel and asphalt roads. Shadows of willow and ironwood limbs by the creek moved on the water like darting fish. It was always that turning of the season that entered their blood—like redhorse entering the creeks.

They'd watch the creeks and wait. The redhorse might be coming from five hundred miles away, but somehow, watching from a bridge or high bank, they could feel the redhorse coming. Once, he remembered, they arrived at night. At least, that's when they were first spotted. Somebody came into The Trading Post and announced them. They'd stopped at the bridge over Newfound Creek and checked the water with a six-cell flashlight. So they'd all ridden down there and shined lights into the slipping water and seen the redhorse moving upstream, cloud after cloud of them. Here and there a silver side would turn and gleam in the light. The shine they'd all been waiting for.

"Don't just reel it straight in," Buddy said. "Let it sink, then pull it up, reel a little, then let it sink back. Up and down, like."

Hmmm. Jennings leaned his rod against a willow and sipped from the flask of Jack Daniels he took from his jacket pocket. Purple worm. He recalled a quick sequence of colors: the red-faced man mixing Sprite and vodka on the tailgate of a red pickup with amber over-the-cab running lights at an auction he'd gone to with Buddy last night. The young pharmacist in Jewell Hill, in his green smock, declaring to someone in a burgundy shirt with a green alligator on it: one thing you can depend on—people are gonna die, and they're gonna need glasses. Not in that order.

Malt does more than Milton can to justify the ways of God to man. The lines from Housman ran through his head. He sipped the Jack Daniels again before putting the flask back in his pocket and returning to casting.

He remembered walking home one night after having been down to the bridge where they'd spotted the redhorse. Peepers called out of the branch. He stood on the porch before going inside, and looked at the sky, clear in the west, with a quarter moon that lit the curve of sky so that it looked like the inside of a mussel shell, pearly blue. And then, from the dark woods, a bird called—a thrush? The sound sprang up like a single blade of grass, then cut toward him through black limbs like a smooth, silver plow point snapping tree roots and turning up dark dirt in a newground. He'd gone on to bed but past midnight he'd suddenly come awake to lie in the dark, alert. Altered in some strange way. Then he'd remembered the bird, how one blade of bird song had turned the hollow of his mind a deep green lapping pool where his thoughts swarmed like shoaling redhorse, their speckled green and silver backs arching out of shallows under willows by the bank.

Next day they'd headed for the creek, fifteen or twenty of them, men, boys, dogs, the same crowd who'd burned tobacco beds together. Headed for the creek and waded out into the redhorse. Old men who wouldn't brave the icy water any longer, and boys who weren't allowed to yet, walked the banks with buckets and burlap sacks. Some came in boots, but most put on a pair of no-account turned up brogans to wade the creek in. And they'd wade into the redhorse and feel for them back up under the bank, by sunken logs and underwater rocks. Their hands would go numb in the first minute but after the first numbness they felt pleasantly warm when they pulled them, red and raw, out of the water, moving always upstream, as mad as the redhorse themselves, grabbling under the banks, feeling the powerful jerk of the redhorse's body, like an electric shock, as their hands closed around them, as they drew them from the water and threw them, all in one motion, making a twisting, flipping, red and white arc, over the willows on the bank, to the old men and boys coming along with buckets and wet sacks.

They'd work upstream maybe a mile, come out of the water, and build a fire to warm themselves, then stand, watching their pants legs steam. Then, after a while, they'd wade into the water again and move upstream. Another stint in the icy water, and again they'd come out and build a fire. Then back again. Until, sometime in the afternoon, they'd come out at a bridge where folks had driven with cars and trucks. And there they'd come slogging and squishing to a final campfire, and clean redhorse a good two hours, working in steaming clothes, up close to the fire. Always it was the same: as they worked, the delicate red fins and silver sides, the shine they reached for with their hands, turned buckets of bloody water, sperm and roe, turned sheen of air sacks floating on bloody water. And the wildness lay within them, like wind abating.—Maybe they had been nothing but bloodthirsty mountain boys, Jennings thought. For what they really chased, the magic, the miracle, they always killed in reaching for it.

"You see that swirl?" Buddy said.

Jennings cast toward it. "You mean, right about there?"

"Bet that's a good one."

Jennings let the lure settle, then lifted it off the bottom. Snagged. No, the line was moving.

"Hit him!" Buddy called.

Jennings pumped the rod hard. His line cut water, hissing, came up into the air, shedding water beads, stood taut, shaggy with wisps of algae, like shirts hung out to dry, then angled off, throbbing like a pulse. His rod tip whipped down hard, then down again. Son-of-a-gun! The bass surfaced, walked on the water, green back, pink gills, shook his head, and sounded.

Buddy came running and stood beside him. "Told you, if you'd just work it up and down. Told you!"

The bass jumped again and sounded, then ran deep for the far side of the pond. Jennings turned it and started working it in. In a moment of wine-like weather, gray barns in the distance, Jennings looked down and glimpsed rain water grown green in a cow track, green as a frog's back. And then the bass surfaced, green-gold. He snaked it onto the bank, where it lay on its side, exhausted, gasping.

"Here," Buddy said, reaching into his hip pocket. "Here's a stringer."

"I don't want to keep him," Jennings said. "Let's put him back. He's only hooked in the jaw. He'll be all right."

"Boy, I'd keep a fish that big—like, three or four pounds."

"No, I'll put him back. All the fun's just in the catching."

Buddy looked around furtively. "Well, maybe you ought to turn him loose and let's get out of here."

Jennings knelt by the water, wet his hands, and carefully slipped the hook from the jaw of the bass. He eased the bass back into the water and held it until it had righted itself, then turned the fish's head toward the center of the pond and gently shoved it off. "What do you mean, get out of here? I thought you said. . . ."

"Still and all," Buddy said, looking first toward the barns, then back to the road where the pickup was parked.

"Still and all what? Don't still and all me!" Jennings said. He didn't walk fast enough for Buddy as they returned to the truck. Buddy went out ahead and stood waiting by the truck. "What's your rush, all of a sudden?" he asked Buddy. He laid his rod in the truck bed and got in on the passenger side. "You scamp," he said, as Buddy started the truck and turned quickly. "You lied to me. You didn't know whether it was all right to fish in that pond or not! Pull another one like that on me, I'll send you packing!"

Buddy winced but said nothing.

"Don't drive so fast, either."

Jennings settled back in the seat. He chuckled to himself. Kids. Well, he'd been one himself. At least, Buddy hadn't run over Jess Teague's turkey!

He took out the flask of Jack Daniels, sipped, and screwed the cap back on. He was still thinking about woods, water, hounds, the redhorse, and the boy he'd been back then. Some of those boys never changed. Some still reached out with their hands, making traps and barbed hooks of their fingers. Well, he hadn't changed entirely. He'd given up the gun but not the fish pole! But he had learned to stand, open and grey and empty as woods in January, not reaching out. He thought ahead to spring. If he stayed on, what would it be like when once again, after all the years, he'd hear wind roaring in treetops? The broom-sage hills would get up and go again, like lions walking in the sun. The wildness entering. The miracle, the magic—the light around the lives of animals, disguising itself as earth, as air and water, as fin, feather, and fur, suppleness, strength and speech. Always changing, turning, twisting, leaping.

What he'd come to live for now were those times, like the moment back there by the pond when all the colors somehow drew things together; times when everything resembled something else. When a road became a river, shadows of birds in flight became a school of fish, and a rush of ink-black words came like redhorse arriving under the bridge at night.

"I'm pretty sure it's all right to fish there," Buddy said. "I know some other people fishes there."

"So now you're only pretty sure," Jennings said. "When you talked me into coming up here, you were completely sure."

"Anyway, we didn't keep the fish."

"Just hush. I'm on to you. You'll not put me in a situation like that again."

Jennings thought he ought to speak sharply to Buddy, but he was actually more amused than annoyed. He liked the boy.

16

Sitting at his makeshift table in the yard, under the sycamore tree, Jennings watched Buddy walk up from the mailbox with an armload of mail. The boy came across the yard and dropped the mail on the end of the table.

"I'm your renter now," Buddy said. "Figured I'd carry your mail up for you."

Jennings glanced at his watch. Five till four. He figured he wouldn't get anything else done today. "Come to pester me, have you, Henry?"

Buddy waved a hand at the stack of mail. "How come you get so much mail? You famous or something?"

Jennings smiled. He was alternately amused and annoyed by this boy.

"I never do get any mail," Buddy said. "You always get a bushel."

"You ever write to anybody, Henry?"

"No."

"Maybe that explains it."

"That what you're always doing—writing to people?"

Jennings turned from his typewriter to the mail. "That's about it, Henry." He sat picking up envelopes, looking at them, and dropping them back onto the table. He opened one, pulled the check out, folded it and stuck it in his shirt pocket.

"You get paid to write to people?" Buddy asked.

"I get paid not to write, Henry. I'm on permanent retainer to the North Turkey Creek Strip Mining and Victim Blaming Corporation. They send me checks for not writing what I know about them." The boy made Jennings feel as if he were being interrogated.

"That's a lie, I bet!" Buddy pulled up a straight-backed chair and sat at the end of the table, his elbows propped, his chin resting in his hands. "I know you write books. What's in them?"

"Medicine, Henry."

"Medicine?"

"Sure, Henry. People die every day because they don't get the medicine in the books I write."

The boy picked up a couple of the letters, studied the return addresses. "Where's Appalachia? You're always getting letters from 'Appalachian this, Appalachian that'."

"Appalachia's where you are, Henry."

"This is Newfound, not Appalachia."

"You don't even know where you are, do you, Henry?"

"I bet Appalachia's over in Virginia somewheres—where you lived before you come back home. Let's go over there sometime. I'd like to see it." Buddy spied Jennings' guitar, propped against the porch railing. "Why don't you play something?"

"Why don't you ask a few questions, Henry?" He'd brought the guitar out of the house at noon and fooled around with it awhile—enough to discover how rusty he was.

"Play something," Buddy said.

"Don't have the heart, somehow, Henry." Which was true.

"Wished you'd play it sometime. You used to play one real good."

"How do you know?"

"Roma said so."

"I did used to play," Jennings said, remembering.

"With my Mama at the Rocky Top Festival," Buddy said.

"That's right—I did."

Buddy sat there looking expectant, as if he wanted Jennings to talk about the Rocky Top Festival and his mother. When Jennings didn't elaborate, he said, "Let's go ride around. We could ride over to Jewell Hill."

Jennings sighed. "I don't want to ride over to Jewell Hill. I go over there, hoping things will look better. They just get worse."

The boy's eyes brightened. "We could check out the flea market!"

"Always the same junk, Henry," Jennings said. "Ceramic birdbaths, flower pots, pink flamingos standing on one leg. A half-acre of pictures, set up on the lot like tombstones, pictures of children with big wet eyes."

"Why don't you ever buy something?" Buddy asked. "You got the money!"

Jennings rolled a half-finished page out of the typewriter and laid it in a folder. "I would if I needed something to keep crows out of the garden . . . coons out of the corn."

"You've not got a garden, or a corn patch, either." Buddy picked up Jennings' guitar and strummed the open strings. "You remember when they had all them stuffed animals, and that big stuffed gorilla? Wonder if anybody ever bought that thing?"

114

"If it stays around Jewell Hill long, they'll make it a deputy sheriff, or a school board member," Jennings said.

Buddy pretended to make chords on the neck of the guitar. "They say the school board wants to close the Kingdom School. I heard Lloyd Sutherland talking down at The Trading Post. You know who's head of the school board? My Uncle Hilliard."

"Yeah, I know," Jennings said.

"They're saying you're in for it—coming back home," Buddy said.

"They're saying that, are they?" Jennings wanted to hear more.

"Yeah. Loafers down at The Trading Post. Dee Rhodommer, Wiley Woolford. That crowd. They set around and talk. Anyway, something I want to ask you—does my Uncle Hilliard run Cordell County?"

"No. Why?" Jennings wondered what Buddy had been hearing.

"Down at The Trading Post I heard Delano Crumm say Hilliard did."

"Well, what does Delano Crumm know? Be careful with that guitar, now."

Buddy leaned the guitar back against the porch railing. "Hilliard acts like he runs everything. That's why I despise him —that and because he made Grandma and Grandpa Shelton move off their place instead of helping them stay, like they wanted to." Buddy gestured toward the barn. "When are you going to put our house back together? It's just stacked up out yonder."

"Soon, I hope, Henry."

"Anyway, I despise Hilliard. Wished he wasn't my uncle. If I had to carry his coffin, I'd drop it!"

Jennings couldn't help but be tickled by Buddy. He turned his chair away from the table and stretched his legs. "Well, if it makes you feel any better, Henry, your Uncle Hilliard doesn't run the county."

"I heard Hilliard got a teacher run off," Buddy said. "Said there was this teacher at Cordell High and. . . ."

"Who said?" Jennings asked.

"I heard it at The Trading Post. There was this teacher at Cordell High and Hilliard went up to him on the street one day, said to him, 'I dreamed last night you bought one of my little houses up in Dogwood Acres,' but the teacher never bought a house up there and wasn't hired back next year."

Jennings had heard that story. He didn't know whether it was true or not. He liked to think it wasn't. It was true that Hilliard dealt more in real estate now than in coal. But he started in coal. Wildcat mines. "Hilliard has a lot of say about things in Cordell County," he told Buddy. "But run the county? No. Hilliard's just a middleman." Hilliard looked powerful to local folks, but he was just a middleman, one of several. The real power lay in two corporations. When they whistled, Hilliard went running with all the others.

"Delano said Hilliard even got you fired from teaching school one time," Buddy said.

There was that story, too. Jennings remembered when it had made the rounds. "I doubt it," he told Buddy.

"Don't you know if he did or not?"

"No."

"If I thought he'd done anything like that to me," Buddy said, "I'd find out for sure, then lay for him and fix him good!"

Jennings laughed. "If Hilliard got me terminated, he did me a favor. That's how I see it," Jennings said. "He helped me make up my mind to go back to *school*." He grinned slyly at Buddy.

"I was wondering how long it'd take you to get around to bringing up school!" Buddy said. "You want to ride around awhile?"

"Don't change the subject," Jennings said.

"I'll drive," Buddy said. "And we won't talk about school."

"I'm busy," Jennings said. "Was, till a feller came by and interrupted me."

"We wouldn't have to go to Jewell Hill. Just ride around, listen to WWJH."

Jennings shook his head. "That station depresses me. Nothing but country music and a police blotter full of wrecks and stolen tape decks." Jennings launched into a mock newscast from the Jewell Hill radio station. "Yewnit 1, driven by Mr. Ernest Honnicutt of Pea Ridge, Route 1, crossed the road, plunged down an embankment, and overturned. Two passengers in Yewnit 2, which struck a culvert in an attempt to avoid Yewnit 1, 18-year-old Dustin Leatherbetter and his wife, 13-year-old Chelsea Leatherbetter, were pronounced congenital idiots on arrival at the Rag Shank Infirmary. Mr. Honnicutt was lodged in the Rag Shank jail on a variety of charges, including driving under the influence of an insane theology, carrying a concealed church key, and littering the public highway with his person. In addition, according to a report filed by Trooper Hooper, the arresting occifer, Honnicutt's fly was unzipped."

"Half the time you don't make a lick of sense," Buddy said.

"Well, you go ahead and stay out of school," Jennings said, "and you can be a part of Jewell Hill society, too!"

"You just make fun of everything," Buddy said. "If all you can do is make fun of things around here, why'd you even come back?"

Jennings gazed thoughtfully at Buddy. Now and then he had no comeback to the boy's questions.

"And you won't ever give a straight answer," Buddy said.

Jennings wanted a drink. "There's not always a straight answer to give, Henry." He stepped inside the house and poured himself a little Wild Turkey in a water glass. " 'Tell all the truth, but tell it slant'—you ever hear of that, Henry?" he said, coming back out on the porch.

"Maybe. Maybe not. There's not any straight answers, like you said!"

Jennings sipped the Wild Turkey. "Not bad, Henry! Not bad. You know, you're like a half-moon, Henry. About half what you could be. I think I'll start calling you Moon."

"Is that Wild Turkey liquor you're drinking?" Buddy asked.

Jennings stared at his glass, nodded.

"Are you going off on a Wild Turkey hunt?"

"No. I've found the Wild Turkey, Henry. I mean, Moon. Or maybe I ought to call you Possum, only a possum's got sense enough to crawl in the pouch till it's big enough to be out on its own. And a school, a school is what a human has instead of a pouch. Yeah. Why do you think a school is called an alma mater? How come?"

"I don't know."

"Because a school's a mother, a nourishing mother, like a pouch with tits for little possums like you."

"There's this girl goes to Cordell County, her name's Alma Wade—boy, she's got 'em!"

"I'm not talking about Alma Wade's tits, I'm talking about school! I swear, the more I try to talk to you, the more I end up sounding. . . ."

". . . . like an idiot?" Buddy said.

Jennings consoled himself with the Wild Turkey. Maybe if he just sat and sipped the whiskey, and said nothing, the boy would leave.

No such luck.

118

"I've been cleaning up my pictures," Buddy said. "You know, the ones the haulers forgot when they took Grandma and Grandpa Shelton's things."

"You better take your pictures on over to Hilliard's and stay with your Grandma and Grandpa," Jennings said.

The boy ignored Jennings. "There's this picture of my Great-Grandpa Shelton," he continued, "and I was trying to clean the glass, and took these little tacks out of the back, and I found this other picture behind my Great-Grandpa Shelton's. I don't know who it could be."

"There's somebody behind everybody, Henry," Jennings said.

"I'd like to know the straight of it," Buddy said. "Grandma Shelton's mama, my Great-Grandma Spivey, she almost got mixed up one time. They went to somebody's house one Saturday night, for a corn-shucking. . . ."

"You told me that story once before, Henry," Jennings said. It was hard to know whether the boy just rambled or whether he knew exactly what he was doing. Anyway, he was making Jennings uncomfortable.

"I've got this other picture," Buddy said, ". . . picture of my Mama. Just a little one." He took a snapshot out of his wallet and showed it to Jennings. "She lives in Ohio. Think it's Ohio. Sometimes she goes to New York."

Buddy kept holding the photo out to Jennings until Jennings felt he should take it. It was Roseanne, all right. Not a recent photograph, surely, but it was Roseanne. In shorts, posing on the hood of a car somewhere, one hand behind her head, trees in the background. Jennings turned the photograph to see if there was a date on the back. There was none. He looked at Roseanne again, then at Buddy, nodded, and handed the photo back to the boy.

"You got any pictures of yourself?" Buddy asked.

Jennings hesitated.

"I know you've got some." Buddy looked around on the table. "I saw some in an envelope. You got one I could have?"

Jennings had four or five dozen black and white photos he sent ahead for publicity purposes when he was scheduled to speak somewhere. "What do you want with a picture of me, Henry? I'm right here, you can see me."

"Put it in my billfold," Buddy said. "With my Mama's." He found the manilla envelope full of photos on the table. "Can I have one?"

"Go ahead, Henry."

Buddy took one and put it in his wallet. "I'm writing a book, too, sort of. You know that?"

What was this boy up to? Jennings wondered. Was he simply trying to impress Jennings, get on his good side? "You're writing a book, Henry?"

"You remember you told me if I was going to live in the woods, like Henry Thoreau, I'd have to keep a journal? Well, I've started writing stuff down—thoughts. But not because of Henry Thoreau."

He'd started writing things down because of something he'd heard at The Trading Post, he told Jennings. There was this man over in Granger County whose Daddy got run over in the road, years ago, about dark, one Christmas Eve.

Jennings knew this story—had a newspaper clipping about it somewhere in one of his many files. He listened while Buddy recounted it.

Whoever ran over the old man didn't stop, Buddy explained, so they didn't know who did it. So this man, the son of the man who got run over, started writing things down in a tablet—exactly what happened. He listened and looked and asked around, and wrote it all down in tablets. For awhile, he figured whoever ran over his Daddy lived right around there—in Granger County. Then he got to thinking . . . it happened on Christmas Eve, so it might have been somebody that used to live around there, and was working off up north now, and they'd just come home, like people did on the Fourth of July, or Thanksgiving—or Christmas. So he wrote down the names of everybody that used to live around there but was working up north now—in Indianapolis, or Cleveland, or Columbus, or Dayton. And he made another list of people who had kin living on the creek above him, because the man's Daddy had been hit by a car that was coming down off the creek. He filled up several tablets, and. . . ."

". . . and finally figured out who it had to be that ran over his Daddy," Jennings said.

"You know about it?"

"And there was a trial and somebody was convicted of the hit-and-run, years after it happened," Jennings said.

"Right!"

Jennings suspected he knew where Buddy was going with all this. Was it possible? "So you figured—what?" Jennings asked.

"Figured if I got me a tablet, and listened, and looked, and asked around—well, someday I might be able to find *my* Daddy."

Just as he suspected. Was it possible that Roseanne, or the boy's grandparents, old Mr. and Mrs. Shelton, hadn't told the boy who . . . ? "Talk to your Grandma and Grandpa about your Daddy, Henry! Write your Mama a letter, instead of writing down stuff in a tablet!" Jennings was irritated by the implications of Buddy's story, his journal-keeping, the way the boy had put Jennings' photo in his wallet with Roseanne's. This boy was already building his case. Good Lord!

Jennings looked at his watch. "Henry, I'm going to drive over

121

to Roma's in a little while. I'll drive you on over to Hilliard's."

"You got a date with Roma?" Buddy asked.

"Sort of. Yeah. A date.—Go on up the holler, get your things together, and I'll take you on over to Hilliard's and you can stay with your Grandma and Grandpa."

"I told you, I'm your renter now," Buddy said. "I'm not going to Hilliard's."

"You'd better. Because I won't be coming back tonight. And won't be here tomorrow or the next day, either."

"You going to Appalachia again, I bet."

"I told you, you're in Appalachia."

"You're going to a college?"

"Yeah. Try to stomp out a little ignorance. Can't stomp out any around here.—You know, you can give a man a fish, that feeds him for one day. But if you can teach him how to fish. . . . That's what I'm trying to do, Henry, teach you how to fish."

"I showed you how to fish a plastic worm. I taught you." Buddy's face brightened. "You want to go fishing?"

"No! I wasn't even talking about fishing!"

"Sounded like it to me.—What do you do at them colleges?"

"I told you, Henry. Stomp out ignorance. A college is a good place to do that. They gather a lot of it in, all in one place. Makes it easier to stomp out, Henry."

"I wished I never had heard of Henry."

"Yes, he is a rebuke to us all," Jennings said.

"Whatever that means." Buddy started down the porch steps.

"You're not going to ride over to your Grandma and Grandpa's?"

"Told you, I'm your renter now!"

Jennings picked up his typewriter and carried it into the house. How was he going to get shed of this boy?

17

As they drove toward Johnson City, Roma was giving Jennings a quiz from *Country Song Roundup*—and looking the happiest he'd seen her look so far, all comfortably settled with her head on the pillow on the passenger side of Jennings' Skyhawk. His cousin Edna Rae had the back seat all to herself.

"This quiz is called *The History of Country Music vs. You*," Roma said.

"Why does it have to be me versus country music?" Jennings asked. "I'm not against country music."

"Hush and take the test," Roma said.

Jennings glanced over at Roma. She was smiling and studying the country music magazine.

"'Hello, Walls' was written by Faron Young.—True or false?"

"False," Jennings said.

Was this really happening? He knew Roma had taken him on, as a project, and was bent on putting him into circulation, as she put it. It was Roma who'd insisted he have the tape deck installed in his car, and wanted him to like country music; who'd put him back in touch with his cousin, Edna Rae. And he remembered Roma having said something, a couple of weeks ago, about going to a Conway Twitty concert. Since he'd come back to Newfound, everything had gotten so complicated—Roma, the boy, Buddy, living on his place in that old tenant house up the holler. And now this trip Roma had arranged to a Conway Twitty concert in Johnson City, Tennessee. What was he doing here? It didn't seem possible it was happening. But it was happening.

"False is right," he heard Roma say. "Faron Young didn't write 'Hello, Walls'. Who did?"

"I don't know," Jennings said. When Roma said "false," his mind, like a dandelion bloom, scattered on her breath. He was floating, floating.

"If you don't know, you only get half-credit," she said.

There on old 23 North, headed for Johnson City, he glanced at Roma again. Her black chinquapin eyes shone with gladness. Gladness, he realized, he wanted to be the reason for. It was simple—what he was doing here. Roma made him happy. If she knew how happy, it would scare her. It scared him. "I want credit," he said to her. "If I got it right, you have to give me credit."

Roma shook her head. "You can't get full credit," she said.

Or rather, he thought, she sang. Everything she said was half song. Sometimes a bawdy song, admittedly.

"This is a two-part answer," Roma explained. "The answers are here upside-down on the page. The first part is false. You got that right. But then it tells who did write 'Hello, Walls'."

This was all so silly, but Jennings liked it. Roma made him happy, made him realize he hadn't been happy in a long time.

Over in that field there, a red barn with a Hester battery sign on it. The barn, even the Hester battery sign, was beautiful, because he was happy, driving along like this with Roma, taking a foolish country music quiz.

"Guess if you don't know," Roma said. Her face was hidden now behind the *Country Song Roundup*.

"Would you repeat the question?" Jennings said. He hadn't forgot. He just wanted to hear Roma talk.

"Who wrote 'Hello, Walls'?"

"Let Edna Rae answer that part," Jennings said. "She'll know."

"Edna Rae, you want to help him?" Roma asked.

"Willie Nelson wrote 'Hello, Walls,' " Edna Rae said from the back seat. So matter-of-fact. Like Pete Rose smacking a single, Jennings thought. He glanced at his cousin in the rear view mirror. Edna Rae's hair was still as blonde as it had been when she was a teenager. But she was in—what?—her middle-fifties now. He wondered if she dyed her hair to keep it looking that way.

"Right!" Roma said. "Willie Nelson is right. But you can't help him anymore, Edna Rae. Jennings has to do it by himself. He claims he's studied up on country music."

"Jennings always was good in his books," Edna Rae said from the back seat. "I remember, when I was in high school, Jennings was just a little feller. Couldn't have been in but about the second or third grade." Edna Rae told how she and Jennings both rode the same bus, and in the afternoon Jennings would come around where Edna Rae would be waiting on the bus with her girl friends and read from their high school books. "And him in only about the third grade," Edna Rae said. "Could pronounce every word right, no matter how long it was. We used to

125

look through our books for the biggest words we could find and get Jennings to pronounce it. And he could. Just stand there in his little overalls and say it right every time."

"Little overalls!" Roma said.

"You remember that, Jennings?" Edna Rae asked.

"I remember how you'd let me sit beside you on the bus, on the big seat," Jennings said. "I don't remember being such a showoff."

"We knowed you'd make something," Edna Rae said.

Jennings thought back over the years. He had done well in college. Then he came back home and taught at Cordell County High. He got interested in what was happening to the county, to the whole region. Strip mining. Pollution. Development. And he began talking about that. Writing about it. Speaking out at the Rocky Top Festival. At the end of his second year of teaching, his contract was not renewed. He'd gone back to school and just kept going until he'd completed graduate school. Turned his dissertation into a book. Taught in a couple of universities. For years now. All the while he'd been writing poems, stories, essays, publishing a book every couple of years. Now graduate students wrote about him.—He'd "made something," as Edna Rae put it. But he wasn't sure what. And now, all these years later, he was still trying to come home.

Roma turned a page in the *Country Song Roundup*. "Now, you can't help him anymore, Edna Rae. We can't find out how much he's learned if you're always helping him.—Here's one. This singer is the seventh son of a seventh son."

"Glen Campbell," Jennings said.

"Heey, that's right!"

"That means he can cure thrash," Jennings said. "Ask me another one."

"The Texas Drifter was: A. Ernest Tubb, B. Bob Wills, C. Goebel Reeves, D. Johnny Bond."

Jennings thought a minute. "Goebel Reeves."

"Right again!" Roma lit a cigarette. "I believe he really has read up," she said back to Edna Rae. "Why, two months ago, when he came home, he didn't know diddly about country music. He really didn't! And he never took any interest in it when he was home years ago, I don't believe. I think he acted like he was above it back then."

Back then, Jennings thought. He knew Roma had in mind what she had already accused him of—being interested only in traditional ballads, the sort of thing he sang with Roseanne Shelton at the Rocky Top Festival.

"How old was Elvis when he died?" Roma said now.

"Piece of cake. Forty-two,". Jennings said.

"Right. But that's too easy. Let's see. . . ."

"We're getting on down the road," Edna Rae said from the back seat. "Couldn't be too far to Johnson City now."

Glad Roma was feeling better than she had the other evening, Jennings said, "We got a soon start. Look at that corn over there. This dry weather's plumb rurnt it. They've not even bothered to take it out of the field."

"I wished you'd listen to him," Roma said. She shifted on the seat, wiggled her shoes off onto the floor and tucked her feet up underneath her. "He's doing it again—talking like he used to. The other day, Edna Rae, he said that old silo at Wellses was out of whanker, like the Leaning Tower of Pisa. Out of whanker! You don't hear people around home, even, say things like that anymore."

"Used to you did," Edna Rae said. "Why don't you just leave that school and come on back home for good, Jennings?"

"I'm thinking I just might," Jennings said.

"Shoot, just do it!" Edna Rae said. "You stay, and we'll run you for school superintendent. Get rid of old lard-butt. He's the dumbest thing, anyway!"

"No, thanks!" Jennings said. "Besides, the Cordell County Schools and I parted company a long time ago."

Coming home is a tricky business, Jennings thought. He remembered sitting in the living room at home a few days ago—the room was still just as his mother had left it—and staring at the picture that had hung on the wall there for as long as he could remember: a tree-lined stream with a rocky shore, the stream flowing toward the viewer. You looked upstream toward mountains soft and misty—and all false, false! The water and blue sky identical, the trunks of trees with only the crudest indication of bark, the leaves undifferentiated. Rocks on the shore like no rocks that ever existed. It was a pastoral twice removed. No, three times. An unnatural nature scene.

He'd sat looking at the picture as if for the first time, thinking it was like the picture of home he carried in his mind—until he got home. Again and again over the years he'd romanticized how it had been growing up here, how it would be to return. Coming home this time, his head full of schemes and projects, he'd already driven past Newfound Church—as if everything were still just as it had been—before he remembered his father's grave—and now his mother's—there on the hill. He wondered about the pictures of life he found in the old songs Roma had reacquainted him with. Were they as false as that picture on the living room wall? And the pictures he'd painted in poems and stories and essays—were they false, too? He thought of Roma, and the pictures of her he carried in his mind. Her voice and laughter, like running water. Was he making pictures of her as false as that one in his mother's living room?—No, he couldn't believe that. Roma was here, in the car beside him. Roma was the genuine article.

Edna Rae had taken a Twitty City brochure out of her purse and was showing it up front to Roma and Jennings. Jennings had read up on Conway Twitty but hadn't come across anything about Twitty City, which he now learned was near Nashville. Edna Rae had never been there but she knew all about it and wanted to go there sometime. There on the brochure was Conway under the Twitty City Banner, and Conway's symbol, the Twitty Bird, wearing a cowboy hat and strumming a guitar, and under that, Conway in a green knit shirt and green baseball hat saying, "Hello, darlin' . . . Nice to see you." Jennings could appreciate the slick glossiness of the brochure as a production, but it seemed rather ridiculous. Twitty City? A Twitty Bird? He wasn't picking up on something.

Jennings winked at Roma. "Let's give Edna Rae a quiz on Conway."

"She'll just make a hundred, I guarantee. She knows more about Conway than Conway's Mama does."

"His Mama lives there at Twitty City," Edna Rae said. "Has her own little house."

"See what I mean!" Roma said.

"Let's try her, anyway," Jennings said. "You ready, Edna Rae?" He glanced at Edna Rae in the rear view mirror. She'd had her hair done for the concert. Edna Rae's long blonde hair had always been her best feature. Jennings could remember, when he was very small, going somewhere with Edna Rae. To a fair, maybe. She had taken him so many places. She was a gangling girl and he had a hard time keeping up with her. Kept getting lost from her, but always he'd find her by spotting her hair. "Conway Twitty's real name is—fill in the blank," Jennings said.

"You'll have to beat that," Roma said.

"Harold Jenkins," Edna Rae said.

"He got the name Conway Twitty from—complete the statement."

"Conway, Arkansas and Twitty, Texas."

"See, I told you," Roma said.

"Maybe I can trip her on a multiple choice," Jennings said. "Conway started out as A. a truck driver, B. a dry point etcher, C. an encyclopedia salesman, D. none of the above."

"None of the above," Edna Rae said. "Because he started out as a baseball player. He owns part of the Nashville Sounds."

"You might as well give up," Roma said. "Edna Rae knows her Conway Twitty."

Roma had been thinking about this trip, it turned out, even before she'd taken him to see Edna Rae that evening a couple of weeks ago. Edna Rae wouldn't ride anywhere with her alcoholic husband Earl anymore, even if she could catch him in good enough shape to drive. She'd been going to Al Anon meetings in Jewell Hill (Roma got her started going), where she learned that she hadn't caused Earl's alcoholism, couldn't control it, and couldn't cure it. The important thing for her was to try to have a life of her own. For Edna Rae, that meant going to see Conway Twitty. So Roma had worked it out.

Edna Rae had been to a concert in Johnson City once before, but that was to see Kenny Rogers, not Conway. Earl had driven her. That was the last time she'd ever gone anywhere with Earl. Edna Rae told about the Kenny Rogers concert while Jennings stopped at a restaurant for coffee and sandwiches. The Gatlin

Brothers warmed up for Kenny. A comedian came out and told jokes. He said he wasn't going to be like a lot of comedians and tell a bunch of dirty jokes; then he told the filthiest jokes Edna Rae had ever heard. But everybody liked it. Then a big cloud of white smoke poofed up on the stage and out of it stepped Kenny. And he did a set. But he was hoarse that night. Then he showed some of his home movies, showed the one of his baby being born. Lord! But everybody liked it!

Jennings grinned and sipped coffee.

Kenny was even hoarser during the second set, Edna Rae said. He cut it short and went offstage. Then the announcer said Mr. Rogers was coming back onstage for an important announcement. Kenny came back out, said he didn't feel right about the show, he was hoarse, as was plain to anybody. "So this one's on me," Kenny said. Somebody would tell folks how to get their refund. Edna Rae never got her refund, though, because Earl wrecked them on the way back to Jewell Hill that night. Almost killed them both. She'd seen enough, anyway. Hadn't expected much from Kenny.

"Kenny don't blow Edna Rae's dress tail up, not like Conway," Roma said.

They drove on toward Johnson City. Edna Rae was getting excited, Jennings could tell, for she was a fountain of information about Conway. Conway had more number one songs in a row than anybody until "Georgia Keeps Pullin' On My Ring" came in second to something by Dolly Parton. It was funny how she still knew Conway's "Georgia Keeps Pullin' On My Ring" but she couldn't even remember Dolly Parton's song. Edna Rae liked some other performers—the Kendalls, the Statler Brothers. She even liked some of Kenny Rogers. But he was too upscale. Edna Rae had met a woman, in the Sears Store in Jewell Hill where she clerked, who'd had three nervous breakdowns because she couldn't be with Conway. Edna Rae thanked the Lord she hadn't gone over the edge herself, but she thought she knew something about what that woman must have gone through, poor thing. You never heard of anybody having nervous breakdowns over Kenny Rogers, though.

Edna Rae was a hoot! Jennings thought. And the closer they got to Johnson City, the more she talked.

18

Considering Jennings didn't know his way around in Johnson City, they got there none too soon. They found the hall and made it to their seats. The show began. They called them concerts, Jennings knew, but this was unlike any concert he'd ever attended. More like a basketball game, fireworks display, and political rally rolled into one. Of course, this was his first country music concert; he hadn't known what to expect.

Jennings listened and watched, incredulous. What was it with this "Hello, darlin' . . . Nice to see you?" The women went wild. He must be missing something. He'd read over the lyrics to a lot of Conway's songs and they'd struck him as slightly ridiculous. Performance didn't much improve them, in his opinion. He had to laugh at "Somewhere Between Her Blue Eyes and Jeans," and when they went out to get something to drink during a break he couldn't resist kidding Edna Rae about the song.

The next thing he knew, Roma, returned from the ladies'

restroom, was coming at him mean and dark, like a storm. "What did you say to Edna Rae?" she wanted to know. "What did you say about Conway."

"Gosh, I don't know. We were talking. What's wrong?"

"Did you say something about 'Between Her Blue Eyes and Jeans'?"

"That dumb song. Oh, yeah."

"What did you say?" Roma shifted her weight to one hip and looked at Jennings defiantly.

"I guess I said I thought the lines were dumb. 'Somewhere between her blue eyes and jeans/Is a heart that lies broken along with her dreams'."

"You think that's dumb, do you?"

"If the location of her heart is that much in doubt, she must be an anatomical freak."

"And that's what you said to Edna Rae?"

"Something like that."

"Well, shit, Jennings!" Roma pulled hard on her cigarette and blew the smoke out. "How come you have to be such a smart ass? Ever think about it? How come?"

"I swear, I didn't mean . . . I was just running on."

Roma's eyes flashed with fury. "That's what was dumb!"

"I just said what I thought about the song. Just the way you and I sit around and talk about songs. Say what we think about them."

" 'Blue Eyes and Jeans' just happens to be the story of Edna Rae's life. You know what her life's been like, what it's like now. Why don't you stop worrying about the fine points and listen to what the song says?"

"Are we going to argue about a dumb song?"

"You've hurt Edna Rae."

"I didn't put Edna Rae down. I put the song down! How did I hurt Edna Rae?"

"I don't believe you, Jennings Wells! If you don't know, I can't explain it to you. She's there in the restroom crying. Try to figure it out!"

"I sure didn't mean to hurt Edna Rae. That's the last thing I'd want to do."

"Well, you did! Made her cry. Ruined her trip! I'll tell you one thing, Jennings Wells, there's some things you can't study up on in two weeks! Conway knows some things you don't!" Roma dropped her cigarette on the concrete floor, stamped it, twisted the sole of her shoe back and forth, and went back into the restroom.

Oh, hell, Jennings thought. He suspected Roma was right. He hadn't researched country music, it had researched him.

He went back to his seat and for the rest of the concert sat like a chastened child in church. Roma brought Edna Rae back from the restroom. He could see she had been crying. Jennings didn't hear much of the second half. He was too preoccupied and contrite. The drive back was some better. At least they talked. But the talk was subdued. Hoping it would help, Jennings said how much he liked Conway's "I've Already Loved You in My Mind." By the time they got back over into Cordell County he thought their talk was returning to something approximating naturalness. He put on a tape of gospel songs. When they got back into Jewell Hill he was singing along on "O Beautiful Star." Edna Rae joined in, faintly. But Roma didn't.

Jennings walked to the door with Edna Rae. He wondered what shape she would find Earl in, but thought he'd said enough. He held his cousin's hands in his and said, "Edna Rae, I'm sorry I smarted off. I've got a lot to learn. Please forgive me." She smiled and hugged him. He felt better—and remembered how, when he was a little boy, Edna Rae would carry him when he was tired or fell down. She was still carrying him.

Jennings sat idling in the drive until Edna Rae had turned on a light in the house. Then he backed out and pulled away slowly. "Help me make it up to her," he said to Roma, who sat in darkness on the passenger side.

He waited for Roma to answer. She said nothing all the way to the house. He pulled up the long drive, pulled in beside Roma's Mercury, and turned off the ignition. They sat a minute in darkness. "Want to come in?" he asked.

"No."

"Will you come by tomorrow?"

Roma opened the door on the passenger side and started to get out. "No."

"I'll come over to your place then."

"No."

"You don't want to see me? Is that it?"

She let the door ease shut and sat in the dark looking straight ahead. "I fell in love with you, Jennings, a long time ago—when you used to come by our house and I danced for you. Sure, I was little, but . . . I've always measured other men by you, at least by what I thought you were. And none measured up. I guess I've been waiting for you—all this time—thinking we could be together." She opened the door again. "Guess I was wrong again."

She was right about one thing, Jennings thought: he didn't belong here anymore. He'd thought he knew this place, but ever since he'd been back he'd been having feelings—he should have understood them better—feelings like—like the pasture field above the barn: grown up in pines too thick ever to enter again. He had to admit it: he didn't live here any longer. Couldn't live here any longer.

She opened the door wide and got out. "I'm going home."

"Well, I'm not!" he snapped, suddenly angry. He got out of the Skyhawk and slammed the door hard. "You know, you're right, Roma. I know about as much about Newfound as I know about country music. You've as much as said it. And Hilliard said it: what gives you the right? he said. It's the ones who've *stayed* here, he said. Buddy said it, too: if all you do is make fun of this place, why did you even come home? Good question. But you've said it best of all. Thanks, Roma."

Roma walked toward her Mercury. She stopped and turned to him. "I know what you're going to do. You'll leave now. Go on! Leave! Get about two hundred miles from here, and you'll be able to like Newfound again. You can think you understand it, and we'll all be nice smooth people—no rough edges. Maybe you can finish your book—about how wonderful it is to be part of some place, rooted. Yeah, you like that word. Kinfolks. Community. You like those words, too.—Goodbye, Jennings Wells."

He walked toward the house as she whipped the Mercury around and sped down the drive. He heard her tires squeal as she pulled out onto the blacktop. God, he wanted to be gone! Wanted to be anywhere but here! Sick! He was sick of leaning silos and rotten-roofed barns and strip mine sites, hills with their tops shaved off.

He went into the house and packed a suitcase, tossed his shaving gear into a shoulder bag, all the while mumbling to himself.

137

19

Now what?

He drove. Got out on the interstate and drove. Scanned late night radio talk shows. Found nothing more interesting than people who had run up colossal debts on credit cards, and a psychologist giving advice on premature ejaculation. He turned off the radio and drove on until, exhausted at three a.m., he stopped at a motel outside Morristown. Now that he was out of the car, he found himself once more wakeful, alert. He clicked through the tv offerings. Weather, a movie, real estate seminar, evangelist. He went to sleep listening to somebody talking about sick building syndrome.

Again, five hours later, he drove. He would have been leaving Newfound today, anyway, he told himself, to make a little talk in Kentucky. Another motel that evening, bourbon and water, newspapers, magazines, notes. And at a Scottish festival in a state park the next day, marking time before giving a talk on the speech of southern Appalachia, he walked about the grounds in a concatenation of bagpipes, mingling with middle-aged men in kilts. There were acres of cars, trucks and vans—from Indiana, Missouri, Ohio. He read bumperstickers: Support Your Local Piper. Honk If You're Scottish. He sat under a tent— behind a man with large pink ears—listening to a lecture on the myth and reality of Bonnie Prince Charley. In a question and answer session after the talk, it became clear that members of the audience preferred the myth to the reality. Old guys in kilts muttered and cast knowing looks at one another when the lecturer—a professor whose work Jennings had seen around in regional journals—suggested that the Scottish Festival itself was an example of people creating a tradition that never existed.

Jennings walked around again, stopping to watch a demonstration of Scottish sheep dogs down on their bellies, herding ducks into a woven-wire corral. It was ironic, the lecturer had said, that sheep dogs were a part of this Scottish Festival, for they were used in Scotland only after the Enclosure Acts forced people off the land, destroying the traditions the festival thought to celebrate.

He stopped by a small lake to contemplate a Loch Ness monster made of black inner tubes floated on wooden boards. Maybe someday, Jennings thought, after the coal is gone from these hills, there will be festivals in the Appalachian coal fields celebrating D-9 bulldozers used to strip mine coal, and continuous loaders that brought coal out of the deep mines.

He stood at the back of a tent listening to a folk singer who longed to go back to the heatherrr hills, for there was no place on earrrth like the homeland of his birrrth. Scotland, he was coming back soon.

The trilled r's struck Jennings as hoaky decoration, the sentiment seemed to him fatuous. Not only was "the homeland of his birth" stupidly redundant, the whole notion of going home, as this song presented it, struck Jennings as a dubious proposition. He'd proved that to himself by going home and running into Roma, Buddy, his cousin Edna Rae, Hilliard Shelton. Maybe he'd been able to deal with Newfound and Cordell County, as a writer, all these years precisely because he'd been somewhere else. Being away from the place gave him a perspective he didn't have when he was there. A perspective, yes, and a freedom.

When he'd come home, over the years, he'd been subjected to sudden weathers, showers of feelings; feelings whose faces he'd forgot, feelings he could enter into only as a stranger might a house once lived in; feelings like gray tobacco barns, empty of all but the sharp fragrance of last year's burley. Lately, for instance, he'd come on feelings that, like a corn planter or cultivator leaning against locust posts in the toolshed at home, hadn't been used for a long time. Experiencing these feelings again was like taking an axe by its smooth helve, or gripping the handles of a plow again. At first he was always a little saddened, aware only of loss, and he remembered once having said to himself: Admit it, you don't live here any longer. You're settled in a suburb, north of yourself.

But when he'd been in other places, he'd realized the sense of loss was at least part illusory. He'd wakened in strange places to a horn's beep, ship's bells, in a rising falling bunk out at sea, to the sound of a strange tongue spoken outside his door—and realized he'd been dreaming native ground. Once he'd had a vivid dream about his grandmother, who could conjure warts, who knew spells to make butter come, to draw fire from a child's burned finger, to settle swarming bees. He'd dreamed of her running under a cloud of swarming bees, beating an empty pie pan with a spoon until the swarm settled black on a drooping pine bough. (Had the dream been set off by the clatter of garbage cans on the New York street below his hotel window?) Anyway, she'd been there in the dream, and nothing seemed lost.

More important than going home, maybe, was how we felt about home no matter where we might be. It might just be. . . .

In the afternoon he gave his talk, in the tent where the morning lecturer had talked about Bonny Prince Charley. He worked through the presentation mechanically—he'd given it many times—all the while thinking that going home had been a mistake. Back on the road later that afternoon he told himself there were plenty of other places. And he wasn't a salmon, bound to return to his birthplace. The more he thought about it, the more he thought he could live in motion, at seventy miles an hour, traveling like this forever, with trees slipping past on either side of his car while the farthest green fields, keeping pace a little longer, fell slowly behind as his grille ate miles of gray concrete or foraged for gnats like a whale in a shrimp bed.

Each evening he would call a different room home. After all, a few days ago back in Newfound, when he'd sat looking out the window at the mountains, it had occurred to him that the trees and fields were falling past the window, that the house was whining like an engine held at seventy. Pulling away from the house one morning recently it had occurred to him that the fields and fence rows back of the house seemed motionless only because they were keeping pace, for it could be that house and field were holding steady like two cars side by side at seventy on an endless interstate. Back in Newfound he only seemed to be in place. He was still traveling, the whole place was traveling through time, and only seemed to stand still.

He drove south on I-75 to the Highlander Center, where he was always welcome. That night, as he lay trying to go to sleep, he kept remembering the time Bill Moyers, the journalist, had come to the center to interview its founder, Myles Horton, for what turned out to be a two-part show called "The Adventures of a Radical Hillbilly." Moyers had hired a local make-up girl who had stood listening while Horton told Moyers the history of the mountain region—where the people came from, what they'd been through, how Appalachia for a hundred years had been the country's guinea pig. Later, during a break, the make-up girl volunteered to Horton as she brushed away tears: "That was wonderful—what you told." It turned out she was from up around La Follette, or maybe Jellico, Tennessee. "Some of those people," the girl said (a girl not unlike Roma, Jennings thought now) "some of those people you told about, they're my people. I've been ashamed all my life. But that was wonderful, all those things you told. Why didn't they teach that when I was in school? I'll never be ashamed again as long as I live."

Jennings had been teaching high school in Cordell County at the time, and spending weekends at the Highlander Center. That girl weeping quietly for joy at what she'd learned about her place and people, had strengthened Jennings in his resolve to try to change things. At the time he was teaching with a fellow, a boy brought up in the mountains, who taught a curriculum of contempt for his place and people, his only thought being to hoist his students up onto the rocky ledge of his own arrogance. Instead of rooting them in their place, his fellow teacher pulled his students up by the roots, as if they were young corn, and left them wilting in the balk. He sold children out of the mountains like Christmas trees.

From that incident Jennings dated his writing about the mountain region. Before that, his efforts had been sporadic and tentative; that girl, weeping quietly, had concentrated his mind. He began to write about Newfound, about Cordell

County. About Vince Edwards, the yellow-fingered amnesiac, still unable to call his own name after he'd been wounded past all recollection by a slate fall in an underground mine. Old Vince Edwards—he'd become a symbol of how people in the region had all been hurt past recollection, past memory of who they were and where they came from, and how they got to be the way they were.

So he'd resolved to change that. He'd vowed to gather people's loudest nightmares, like dark blooms of thunder, like the inner bark of limbs of lightning. He'd vowed to dig and dry the crooked roots of memory, and brew bitter teas to be drunk to the dregs of knowledge. He'd keep the sweetest recollections, like elderberries and wooly mullein leaves, as medicine, as tonic, past their season, so his people in the mountains wouldn't linger, paralyzed, hurt beyond remembering, unable to speak their name, under a vacant sky.

It was that resolve that had been back of the books, the articles, the essays, the letters in newspapers over the years. All of it written, as Roma had pointed out, from other places. There was no denying that his attachment to his homeplace was heightened by being away from home.

He remembered a trip with another writer, to the Yucatan. That country. Not a single stream on the whole peninsula. But birds poured like a black river down into the cenote, a dark hole of death and bad water, in Libre Union. He remembered the unpainted huts with doors the same acrylic blue as monuments in the cemetery (even death appeared festive). And the godawful marimba music tumbled, like jumbled melons and mangoes. Both life and death wore green, or orange, or red, or all colors together, a screaming cockatoo print of leaves and fruits, and smelled half-rotten, like the marketplace.

The language there in the Yucatan was full of sighs and

breezes, all vowels full of fluff, sounding as if people were saying *yellow, yellow.* He hungered for consonants, strong frames and structures over which vowels were stretched like drying skins. Words like blood, bone, rock, stone.

In the Yucatan he'd thought of his countryman, Jesse Stuart, who liked to build with words, who'd thought a few well-chosen words would outlast cities. Down there, in Mayan country, Jennings had wondered if Stuart could have been so confident about the durability of words, there where though you built with words like blocks of stone, where cities might grow up around your words, and crowds surround them during festivals, you also saw how time, like grass and trees on a Mayan temple, could break your weathered words apart and scatter them like stones across a jungle field.—All the same, the Yucatan country served only to remind him of his native place and people, and made him long for Newfound and crave the crunch and crack of ice underfoot.

He stayed three days at the Highlander Center and then drove away not knowing where he would go next. He was running, he knew. He was adrift. In the evening he drew up to the Hindman Settlement School in east Kentucky. (What was he doing, he asked himself, revisiting his old haunts? Marking time? Waiting for a decision about what to do?)

A contingent of educators from India were visiting the Settlement School. He talked with them at dinner. Afterwards one of the group, a poet/scholar from New Delhi, gave Jennings a copy of his book, a commentary on the *Bhagavad-Gita.* The Settlement School, like the Highlander Center, always had a place for him, and in his room that night he studied the book, which its author had volunteered would improve Jennings' spiritual state.

He spent several hours with the book, being reminded how

sensual and base he was, how bound he was to matter and illusion. Well, yes. He knew he'd never be a sage of steady mind,
because he couldn't withdraw his senses from certain beautiful
objects in the world—as if he were a tortoise and could pull his
head inside his shell. He wondered what Roma was doing.

The more he read the more he grew impatient with the book.
He already knew inaction often disguised itself as action, for
he had sat on boards and committees. And he knew that what
passed for inaction was often quite productive, for he had loafed
and whittled in his time. But when he worked, he couldn't
overcome a knavish attachment to succeeding at the job, or his
miserly inclination to be rewarded for his efforts. According to
the book, he was therefore held in bondage to his work. He admitted, though, that he liked it just that way. According to the
book, this was even worse.

He talked back to the book, filling its margins with comment.
When he heard good bluegrass—not just any bluegrass, but
good bluegrass—or a peewee's call, he didn't want to pass from
delusion's forest. If he had to be indifferent to good bourbon
(Roma liked Jim Beam, he remembered), or pepper, or wood
smoke, then, by God, he'd stay in the woods. Out fishing on
Laurel Lake with Roma he feared he'd always be disturbed by
the flow of his desires, like a boat swept over water by a breeze.
He rather liked being carried away like that, he wrote in the
margin of a page.

Still, the book insisted he was inferior and unwise to grieve
over the dead or lament for the living. All right. He was resigned, for he despaired of ever being able to cross the ocean
of misery and pleasure on the ship of transcendental knowledge. He was resigned to his greed, ignorance and impurity,
his weakness for pungent foods that the book said moved the
passions. The closest he ever came to enlightenment was when

it seemed to him there was a friend walking with him. Was this the Oversoul?

And then from time to time he thought he could see one un-divided nature behind the innumerable forms. And he'd tried to show his vision in a likeness. Sometimes that made a poem. But he never could achieve that California of uninterrupted enlightenment. Always he returned to the laurel hells and dirt roads of his senses, craving smoked ham and red eye gravy.

But, dammit, he also knew a hawk from a handsaw, and always would insist upon the difference. He had no wish to conquer his own mind, but wanted to live with it, as with a cantankerous neighbor, arguing about line fences. In the dark-ness of his senses, a spiritual frog, he didn't desire the kiss of an eastern princess to translate him into a noble soul.

Traveling in a book was no different from traveling to the Yucatan. Both only heightened his awareness of his own par-ticular self. He felt more like a southern mountaineer in the Yucatan than in east Tennessee, more a Brier when reading the *Bhagavad-Gita* than when listening to radio evangelists while driving.

He stayed three days at the Settlement School, and then drove to Valhalla, South Carolina where he stayed two days with a former colleague who'd dropped out of university teaching to become a fishing guide. He'd arrived just right for the fall fish-ing. He sped up and down the lake in a runabout. The first night there he found money in his dreams. In the waking world yellow leaves blew down like coins from hickory and walnut trees onto the lake surface, where green-and-gold backed bass fought one another for his silver spinner.

Another night he lay for hours thinking of Roma and how, if

things had gone differently, he could still be lying with his head in the lap of that springfed woman, who'd given him the gift of her affection. He remembered her voice, now Amazing Grace, now Betty's Being Bad, her love now white water rafting, now a quiet bay.

Fishing again the next day, he thought constantly of Roma and Buddy. Fondly he remembered other autumns, back home —remembered how once, fishing a lake there, Canada geese dropped like a whirring feathered shaft, from a sauterne afternoon sky to the lake's bullseye. That night a speckled bird descended from dreamt sky, walked up to him and spoke: "God found your father in a field."

And he awoke remembering an old man's story, and wrote it down: walking once with friends on a Sunday morning in March, the old man, then a young man, saw a flock of redbirds alight in willows by the creek. The old man and his friend counted five hundred redbirds—and then stopped counting, and made a solemn vow to tell no one, since no one would believe them.—Half a century later, thinking maybe Jennings would believe him, the old man had told him the story.

Jennings had believed him. And now he believed again, half dream, half waking recollection. The story seemed more believable now than ever before. Why shouldn't he believe—when a woman like Roma had fallen like a leaf into his life, and touched him with her hands and heart, a perfect woman he loved for her sweet talk and floating dreamlike face blissful by firelight—this was how he remembered her now—why shouldn't he believe five hundred redbirds in willows by a creek?

He had run, he'd drifted, he'd driven, thinking that somehow he'd work through the whole business. He had been on both

147

sides of the issue, leaving, staying. He had argued with a book, and with his own recollections! And still he didn't know what he should do.

He ought to talk to Roma. Try to, anyway. There had to be a way.

Then, two weeks after going to the Conway Twitty concert with Roma and his cousin Edna Rae, two weeks to the day after he'd left Newfound in darkness, he realized while driving late in the afternoon that he'd dropped off the interstate and was headed back in the direction of Newfound.

20

He made it to Newfound in the early evening and drove straight up the Green Valley Road to Edna Rae's. She was at home alone; Earl, she reckoned, was in Jewell Hill. Standing hangdog under the porch light, Jennings apologized to her for whatever he'd done to hurt her the night of the Conway Twitty concert. Edna Rae took him by the arm and invited him in, insisting he owed her no apology. She knew Jennings never intended to hurt her feelings. She owed him an apology for the way she acted. Edna Rae made it so easy.

Had he been by Roma's? Edna Rae wanted to know.

No, he'd just got back and he'd driven straight here.

Then Jennings didn't know about Buddy?

Buddy? What about him?

Why, Edna Rae said, Buddy had taken sick while Jennings had been gone, while he was living there in the old Gudger house up the holler there from Jennings' house. And the way Roma told it, Buddy had come down to Jennings' house in the night, that night they'd come back from the concert in Johnson City, wanting aspirin for a headache, and he'd banged on the door and sat on the porch, wrapped in an old quilt, thinking Jennings would eventually come. But the way they figured it, Jennings had already left. And Buddy had sat there till way up in the morning the next day, sick and shivering, wrapped in an old quilt. Sometime that day he'd walked to Roma's, or maybe caught a ride, and when Roma had come home from work that afternoon, she found him on her doorstep. Turned out he had hepatitis, what Edna Rae had always called yellow jaundice. Roma said he'd probably got it from drinking bad water. Roma said the water in half of Cordell County was polluted and there was a lot of hepatitis going around.

Jennings nodded. Roma was right. He remembered his encounter with Hilliard Shelton, in Hilliard's office, soon after he'd come home, back in August. He'd reminded Hilliard then of the water problem, but Hilliard had dismissed the notion, maintaining Cordell County had plenty of water, good water.—Anyway, Jennings guessed Buddy had finally gone on over to Hilliard's, to stay with his grandparents.

No! Edna Rae said. Buddy had vowed he'd never go to Hilliard's. Roma had taken him in. He was staying at Roma's.

Jennings considered this turn, and how his having been gone when Buddy got sick had made things worse. He'd hoped being able to tell Roma that Edna Rae had forgiven him—he'd hoped that would smooth things out between him and Roma. But now she'd hold it against him that he'd been gone when Buddy got sick, making it harder to get back on her good side.

It was as if Edna Rae were reading his thoughts, for she urged him to go see Roma and Buddy.

If he went over there, Roma would probably slam the door in his face, Jennings figured.

No, Edna Rae said. Roma wasn't that way. Edna Rae was confident Jennings and Roma could work things out. And they ought to.

But he didn't go by Roma's. Wasn't up to it just yet. Besides, he didn't want to go unexpected. First, he wanted Roma to know he was back home. And she probably knew five minutes after he left Edna Rae's, he thought, smiling to himself. He bet Edna Rae was on the phone to Roma before he was out of the driveway.

He drove on home, slept, and was answering accumulated mail the next morning when Lloyd Sutherland came by in his ancient pickup. Lloyd Sutherland, from over in that community called The Kingdom. Jennings brought a chair down off the porch and they sat in the warm October sun by Jennings' worktable.

Lloyd had been looking for Jennings for a week now, he said, driving by just about every day, but hadn't seen Jennings' car at home until today.

"I've been—traveling," Jennings told him.

"Well, we heard you'd come home, and different ones down at The Trading Post claimed they'd seed you, then you was gone again, nobody knowed anything about you."

"How are things over in The Kingdom?" Jennings asked. He wanted to get past his unexplained absence, his unpredictable coming and going.

"Ah, Lord," Lloyd said, pushing back his old black hat and running his fingers through his gray hair. Lloyd was—what?—sixty-five by now, maybe pushing seventy, Jennings figured. "You ought to see what they've done to us. It's a sight, I tell you!"

"What's going on, Lloyd?"

"It's the mining," Lloyd said.

"I didn't think anybody in The Kingdom would let their land be mined," Jennings said.

Lloyd shook his head from side to side. "We won't. But they've been stripping over in there on Lost Creek, back of us. And now the hill between us and where they've stripped, hit's just blowed out. Like it'd been dynamited!"

"They're using dynamite?"

"No. You see, what it is, back in there behind us, they've built up a dam and let a whole holler stand full of water. And the pressure, I reckon, just caused the hill in there above us to blow out—in four, five, Lord, I don't know how many places. Acid water's running out of the hill in all these places, like wet weather springs."

Jennings thought of Hilliard Shelton again, remembered how Hilliard had said there was plenty of water in Cordell County, good water. He thought of Buddy and the hepatitis outbreak and remembered now having read a newspaper account of the problem.

Lloyd Sutherland sat, his hands clasped in his lap, working his fingers back and forth in agitation. The water running down was black water, acid water, running down into the branch. It was killing the little minnows and crawdads, even. Couldn't nothing live in that black water. Why, that water would rot horses' hooves, eat the fenders off your truck. You couldn't hardly stand to smell it, even.

"I remember your springhouse, Lloyd, from when I was a boy," Jennings said. And he did, suddenly, vividly. Lloyd had headed his spring out of rocks and run water into the springhouse, into a big stainless steel vat. Five hundred gallon vat. People claimed it was the best water in Cordell County, and would come distances to see Lloyd's springhouse and drink the water. Jennings remembered how when you opened the springhouse door the sight of the water shimmering in the stainless steel vat would momentarily blind you.

Now, Lloyd said, that spring didn't run clear anymore. They had to catch water in pans and buckets, jugs—whatever—and let it set, let it settle out before they could use it. And still it was dingy, not fit. Now, on top of the water business, there was talk of shutting down The Kingdom School. Lloyd and his neighbors had followed what Jennings had written in the paper about mining and the whole situation in Cordell County, and he'd come to see if Jennings could help them, to see if there was any law to get the mining stopped on Lost Creek, or drain that water out—something. Lloyd and his neighbors didn't hardly know how to go about it, didn't know lawyer words.

"I'm not a lawyer, Lloyd," Jennings said.

No, but Lloyd figured Jennings knew the lingo, the book way to go about helping them not only with the mining and the water situation but he hoped Jennings could help them keep their school, too. What Lloyd feared was that the school board people would hold a meeting in Jewell Hill and run something through before folks in The Kingdom knew anything about it. Lloyd had tried to find out when the school board would meet and thought he'd been given the runaround.

Hilliard Shelton was chairman of the school board, Jennings said.

Yes, Lloyd knew he was.

"I went to The Kingdom School," Jennings said. He was thinking out loud. "We all did back then. The Kingdom School *was* the school."

Yes, before the roads came in and things changed, Lloyd recollected. Lloyd studied his gnarled hands and allowed things weren't like they used to be. The young generation was coming up different. His son Fain was back home Christmas, from California, with his wife and younguns. And one of the boys got to playing with a seashell there at home, a seashell they'd always used for a doorstep. And Lloyd had told the boy, Hold it up to your ear, and the boy did, and Lloyd had asked him, What do you hear? Lloyd's grandson had looked at him, grinned, and said, The freeway?—"Now, me and you, we know you hear the ocean roar in a seashell," Lloyd said. "But that boy of Fain's. . . ." Lloyd shook his head. "The freeway!" Lloyd Sutherland stood and adjusted his black hat.

"I'll see what I can do to help," Jennings said.

"We'd all be much obliged."

Editor

Cordell County Courier

I saw in last week's paper that we have an optometrist in Jewell Hill and he's opened up a Mountain Vision Center. Good news. This announcement got me to thinking—about opening up a Mountain Vision Center of my own—of a slightly different kind.

Certainly there's a need. Love is blind. Justice sits winking in the jury box. Men undress mountains with their eyes. Dollar signs catch the eyes of children—and hold on. Some folks are so farsighted they can't see now for later. Others can't see later on for now. Few see farther than ridge-to-ridge. I knew a Cordell County girl who suspected the ocean was a tall tale.

Nobody sees any way out. If you take a backward glance in Cordell County, you're apt to step out in front of a coal truck.

People see smokestacks in their neighbors' eyes, but not the strip mines in their own.

So many folks see double: one eye squints, so they can like themselves; the other wanders, looking about to see if other people like them. Some have no eyes at all, as best I can determine, see everything with someone else's.

A lot of people see through everything—and into nothing. Out looking for the woods, they walk into trees, and over high walls.

I picture myself standing in my Mountain Vision Center, in a white lab coat, like an actor in an ad for aspirin, pointing to the writing on the wall.

I wouldn't post bare facts, the naked truth. Blind in the blizzard of their senses, dazzled by the light of now, most people would only look away, shading their eyes with a hand.

Anyway, facts are like a woman: never so naked as when seen beneath a revealing dress.

The trouble is, most things we see every day, and things we say, we never really see or hear at all. But if we read them. . . .

The trick is to show familiar facts—but caught up in a vision that makes them strange and new—that way of looking that makes a cloud against blue sky a whale on the ocean.

People like play-acting, tricks and sleight-of-hand. If I can work with a needle convincingly enough, I can make people see the thread that isn't there.

Instead of charts with letters large and small, I'll put up newspapers, poems, and stories. I'll post the news, then have people read it off to me. I'll have my patients add up poems and stories, and legal notices of intention to mine, like columns of figures, and so count all the sums they are.

I'll recommend exchanging rose-colored glasses for poems

that make gentle contact with the mind's eye, like a soft lens, lining up then with now, now with then, news of the day with news that stays news, like front and rear gun sights.

I'll have folks step through the door of a poem or story, as if into a dark projection room. Like children running back and forth in front of a beam of light, they'll see leaping shadows of themselves, their own dark shapes on a screen.

If people can become visible to themselves, the things they see and say every day, without surprise, will astonish them.

Somebody's eyes will narrow with suspicion—suspicion that something different from what seems to be happening is actually going on. Something . . . a shape that has no name. Then someone will name the shape. Then everyone can see it who can say it.

They'll see the hand that's supposed to guide everyone's self-interest, invisibly, is tipping over mountains, scooping up land, and reaching into their pockets. They'll see they're dangling from strings held by that hand; they'll see the hand has a face and corporate body, and sits in a board room tapping its foot to the jig they dance.

They'll see they're moving along a mountain road at sixty minutes an hour, into a future that's a mirror with no glass. There's nowhere to pull over, and cars are lining up behind them honking.

They'll see the future has entered them a long time ago, and all this time has been transforming them.

They'll see that the longest memory also sees the farthest up ahead.

Maybe they'll see that sitting down in the evening and looking into the distance is religion, too.

Robert Jennings Wells
Newfound

After Lloyd Sutherland left, Jennings went into the house, poured himself a cup of coffee, and came back out to his work-table. He sat considering all the years, the past two weeks, Lloyd Sutherland's visit, and re-reading the tongue-in-cheek, high-handed letter he'd been about to send to the county paper. He thought of Roma, what she'd think of it. Smart ass, she'd say. He couldn't send it. He was beginning to see how he must have struck people with the letters and articles he'd been sending the paper over the years. He must have sent dozens, maybe hundreds throughout the years he'd been away. He guessed people considered him a village crank. How would this piece of whimsy help Lloyd Sutherland and the folks over in The Kingdom?

Once he had thought seriously of coming back to Newfound and trying to set up some sort of alternative school or center. Now he cringed at the condescension in his mock proposal for a Mountain Vision Center, at its monstrous assumption that he knew what was best for other people. He could halfway understand why people like Hilliard, confronted with such a screed, would say, "What the hell is this? What does it have to do with anything?"

People like Lloyd Sutherland were well aware of their problems. They didn't need someone like Jennings to frame issues for them. They needed people like him to help them *do* something about the problems. He remembered Myles Horton at the Highlander Center telling how once, when he was holding a workshop for striking workers, one man in his frustration pulled a pistol out of his pocket, held it behind Horton's ear, and said, "Goddammit, you're gonna tell us what to *do!*"

People wanted ideas—were sometimes desperate for them.

Jennings was supposed to have them. Well, he did have all kinds of ideas. And surely seeing things not just as they were but as they might be, and seeing into things, the way things were connected—that was vision. But bringing that vision to bear on Lloyd Sutherland's problems. . . .

Lloyd hadn't held a gun to Jennings' head, but might as well have. Lloyd was saying, in effect, "You've got to tell us what to *do!*"

Now, faced with a real situation, he wasn't sure what he should tell Lloyd to do, what he could do to help. Standing so close to the situation, it was as if his vision had shattered.

21

Jennings was sitting at his worktable out in the yard, a sheet of paper rolled into his typewriter, considering what he might say on behalf of Lloyd Sutherland and Lloyd's neighbors in defense of The Kingdom School (he'd found out a school board meeting was scheduled in a week), when Buddy walked into the yard. Pale. Peaked. Carrying more mail from Jennings' mailbox.

"Didn't you pick up your mail when you come back?" Buddy asked, dropping the mail on the end of Jennings' worktable.

"What say, Henry?—Sure, I picked it up. What you've got there is more mail. Must have come yesterday."

"You sure get a lot of mail.—Where've you been, anyway? Been gone two weeks!"

"Been off stomping out ignorance, Henry. Couldn't stomp out any around here."

"You been over to Appalachia, I bet."

"That's right, Henry. And I'm still there."

"No you're not. You're here."

Jennings laughed to himself. "I hear you've been sick, Henry."

"Real sick. Yellow jaundice, they say. But I'm getting better, getting my strength back. I got weak as a kitten.—How'd you know I've been sick? Roma tell you?"

"Edna Rae told me. I've not talked to Roma. Yet."

"You ought to. When I got sick, I walked all the way over to her house. She's got all your books and I've been reading them.—You mad at her or something?"

"We had a—misunderstanding, Henry."

"She's not mad at you. Well, a little, maybe. But she talks about you." Buddy grinned. "Got me checking to see if you've come back home!"

"Is that so?" Jennings said. He picked up the mail Buddy had carried up from the box and started looking through it.

"Guess I'm not your renter anymore," Buddy said.

"I'm glad to hear that, Henry," Jennings said as he opened an envelope with a pencil tip. "I told you you wouldn't last up there in that old house till the snow flies."

Jennings scanned the letter, a two-page, single-spaced ramble from an anthologist who was proposing a collection of essays that would include one by Jennings. There was a permission form to sign and send back in a return envelope. He could see out of the corner of his eye that Buddy was on the verge of saying something. "I can't right now, Henry. I'm busy."

"Can't what? I didn't say anything!"

"But you're about to say, 'Let's ride around.'"

"I was not," he grinned. "I was gonna say, 'Let's drive somewheres.'"

"I've got you figured, Henry," Jennings said.

"Besides, it's Sunday," Buddy said. "Good time to drive around."

160

"Sunday?" Jennings had lost track of the days. Buddy was right; it *was* Sunday.

"Well, Roma's afraid to let me drive her car, and I'm getting out of practice. Don't you need me to drive you somewhere?"

"No."

"I could take you on a Wild Turkey hunt. You could drink Wild Turkey, like you used to before you left out, and I could drive you around."

Jennings signed the permission form, folded it, and slipped it into the return envelope. He did need to drive over around Lost Creek, look the place over. Maybe go past The Kingdom School, take a look.

"I could drive you around, and we could come back by Roma's. That way, I wouldn't have to walk home. I'm not supposed to get too tired because I've been sick."

They drove over to Lost Creek in Jennings' father's old red pickup with the blue right front fender. He'd known the strip mining was going on here; still, he wasn't prepared for the sight. Dear Lord, a whole ridge shaved! As if some knob-knuckled medieval barber, wearing a bloody apron, had operated on a mountain top. He sipped his Wild Turkey. What fat-fingered surgeon made these deep incisions in the living hills—hills that, according to the psalm, went skipping like lambs? They hung now, bleeding toward the creek, like mutton on meat-hooks.

It was Sunday, but the coal trucks were hauling. And a knobby-tired silver pickup passed them, coming down from the operation—a fancy pickup with an over-the-cab lightbar/spoiler and stirrup steps. Jennings glimpsed two sideburned young men in the cab and thought: horny boys smelling of after shave, knives sheathed on the sides of their boots, out looking for slash. He thought of himself and his cousin Gerald, years ago. He thought of boys he'd known who'd grown up in coal camps. Matthew Bays, for instance, who'd grown up at Hardburly. The name of the place told how life was there, in those days. Matthew had been jerked up hard in a deep holler where smoke from the smoldering gob pile hung in air that smelled like carbide and warm dishwater. Hardburly bullies roamed the camp. Their fists broke Matthew's teeth before he worked clanking shifts of hard coal seams and slabs, bolting the dripping roof of gray jack rock. That roof rock fell on Matthew Bays when the mine blew (Jennings remembered it as one of the worst mine accidents in Cordell County). It must have been hard, dying in the Hardburly mine, smothering in the dark. Even the burial was hard, for when they dug the graves of the miners killed in that underground explosion—Matthew Bays and four others—graves in the cemetery on the rocky knoll above the Hardburly coal camp, they'd had to shoot the graves first with dynamite.

"You're talking to yourself," Buddy said.

"I'll show you where I went to school," he said, and he directed Buddy to drive him past The Kingdom School, a red-brick 1–12 school built by the Works Progress Administration during the Depression.

"I went to school there too," Buddy said.

"And you ought to still be going," Jennings said.

"Can't no more. Kingdom School just goes to eighth grade."

"That's right. I forgot."

"If The Kingdom School still had high school, I'd still be going, I guess," Buddy said. "Kingdom School's a good school. But after the eighth grade you have to go to Cordell County High now, and I won't go to that school."

"You'd better.—Slow down along here, then stop at the school."

"Cordell County's not fit to go to," Buddy said.

The Kingdom School appeared to Jennings to have held up well. He remembered his first day of school there; his teacher, Miss Briggs; a war bond rally held there when he was in first or second grade—his father took him along; a guest entertainer from North Carolina, Virgil Gentry, a man with salt-and-pepper hair and thick black eyebrows, who stood on the stage unaccompanied, his hands behind his back, and sang "Barbara Allen." He remembered how the ballad had made his blood run cold—what Emily Dickinson meant by "zero at the bone." The ballad had sounded like many of the poems his Grandmother Wells had recited in the parlor, or the old songs she sang in the kitchen, but Jennings had never felt the real power of the old poems and songs until he'd heard Virgil sing. That had been an evening that had permanently altered him, turned him in a direction he'd been going ever since.

He had his regrets about The Kingdom School. He'd often wished that the images of people he got from books in The Kingdom School had had more to do with his own experience. He recollected that a story about Laplanders, who herded reindeer, seemed closer to what he knew than all those episodes of Dick and Jane and their dog Spot. He remembered reading and re-reading the story about Laplanders until the pages were ready to fall out of the book. Well, the school had provided him with something, finally, that interested him. But the Laplander story was an isolated and memorable high point in his early schooling there. Finding materials that excited students ought to be a daily experience.

A series of recollections from his childhood and adolescence attending The Kingdom School rushed through his mind. Now it occurred to him that his growing up had some of the bleakness of *The Last Picture Show*. Viewing that film long ago he'd been afraid, during several scenes, that lights were going to come up in the theater, a spotlight would discover him, and Ralph Edwards would step out proclaiming, "This is your life!" Most of the time, though, his life here had been as wholesome as *The Waltons*.

Still he wondered if he really sympathized with Lloyd Sutherland and his neighbors, or wanted to keep the school open merely because he had attended it, because it was so much a part of his recollections.

They drove on and wound up at Druther's in Jewell Hill where he bought Buddy a sandwich and a drink at the drive-through window. Jennings looked over the crowd at the fast food restaurant while Buddy played the radio in the pickup. A steady coming and going of cars and trucks. Circling, scratching off. Returning. Who were these people? Were they always here when he was growing up? Did he not remember things the way they were? On the way back to Newfound, as they passed the Little Dove Old Regular Baptist Church, a picture floated into Jennings' mind. How could deity as a dove be heard over that Druther's crowd's approval of the slam dunk, over the paid voice on the radio praising the doublewide, the wine, the water bed?—Or nest where trees fell before knobby tires, and lay down ahead of steel tracks?

He thought of Sundays as he had known them here. His mother in her black dress, a church bell's wider and wider ringing, the sound spreading like ripples over the still pool of Sunday morning. Sunday mornings were the smell of sweat, soap and vanilla, and the morning air on his hot cheek cool as the touch of polished marble gravestones. When they sang in church it seemed the ridge tops and hollows rose and fell around

164

them. And high overhead the church house creaked like an old ship's rigging. They sailed in a storm of hymns, slammed to the trough, rolled to the crest of sermons. The cemetery trailed in the church's wake, with its acre of gravestones like heaving, ringing buoys.

But that was another country. This Sunday's Lord had to be a heavy-duty deity with cruise control and headers, equipped for all terrain, with four-in-the-floor, ram-it jam-it power, a Lord who spoke through an air horn, who bore down on you with Big-feet and a hood ornament whose chrome boobs split the wind. This Sunday's Lord wore a flight jacket, loaded his own shells, hunted doves every fall and moved heaven and earth fifty weeks a year. His only commandment: Thou shalt mention my name a lot—when you're scared, bored, happy, or just plain pissed. It paid to advertise.

"You're talking to yourself again," Buddy said, looking over at Jennings.

"I have a lot to say to myself," he told Buddy. And what he had to say was that, no matter how much this place irritated him sometimes, he was stuck with it. He couldn't change his past, or where or what he came from. You had to affirm your place and people not always because of but sometimes despite. Whatever was rich in the lives of our people enriched us, for we were sprung from the moist ground of their lives. Where they were manipulated in their pride and independence, ex-ploited, tricked out of timber, land and coal, we stood robbed, too. Where they burned, plowed, and mined in ignorance, we were impoverished. Where they cut the future down, we were naked in our present. What they did in their private and collec-tive darknesses was our dawn along a polluted river. Were we doing any better than they did? What notes were we writing for our children? God help us! No, we couldn't separate ourselves

165

from the lives of our people, except through delusion. Our lives flowed from theirs as from a place where two creeks meet: if one came tumbling muddy and trash-filled, the other entered quiet and clear.—Suddenly he was aware that Buddy had turned left on the Sugar Creek Road. "Where are you heading?" he asked, but he already knew.

"To Roma's," Buddy said.

"Then stop at the mailbox. You can walk on over from the road," Jennings told Buddy.

"Can't you stop and stay a while?"

"Roma won't want to see me."

"She will! She does—I guarantee!"

"No.—Maybe I'll call her when I get home."

And he did. Under the pretext of inquiring about Buddy. Did Buddy get home all right? Was he getting better? All the while trying to gauge her tone. She didn't seem hostile, but not exactly warm, either. Sort of—distant, as if she were talking to him and watching tv at the same time.

He was sorry about the Conway Twitty concert debacle. He guessed she'd been right. He'd been so stupid. He'd been by to apologize to Edna Rae, and things were fine between him and Edna Rae. Edna Rae wasn't holding a grudge.

That was good.

He was sorry about leaving, without a word. At the time, it seemed the thing to do.

Yes, it must have.

Looking back on it now, he wondered why his first impulse had been to leave, instead of trying to work things out.

She hadn't been surprised, actually. She figured Jennings

was the kind of person who tried to solve problems by running away from them.

No, he didn't think so.

She'd expected him to leave. If he hadn't left over the Conway Twitty incident, then he would have found some other excuse, she figured.

Why did she say that?

Well, she suspected he considered her a coyote date.

A what kind of date? What was that again?

You know, you wake up in the morning with your arm asleep and you're so horrified by the person lying beside you, on your arm, you'll chew your arm off to get away without waking them.

He laughed into the phone. That was good, Roma!

She laughed—faintly. Well, it was the truth.

No, she was right about a lot of things. She was shrewd. But she was wrong about his thinking she was a coyote date.

She didn't answer. He rattled on: he'd never heard of a coyote doing it, but he knew muskrats and mink would twist a foot off to get out of a trap. Had she read his poem about a three-legged dream? It took off from that notion?

Of course, she had read all his poems.

Well, he felt three-legged, maybe he had twisted a foot off, but he'd like to try, three-legged though he was, to shuffle and stumble back in her direction.

When he hung up, he figured he had made only modest progress toward a reconciliation. He had miscalculated. Fifteen minutes later Roma's headlights raked the front of the house as she turned at the edge of the yard. He was standing in the open doorway when she opened the car door and released country music into the October evening. She came up onto the porch and stood in the light holding something out to him. A rusty leg-hold trap with—what was that in the jaws? A leg off a doll. A Barbie doll? No, a Ken doll, of course!

"This yours?" she asked.

22

Buddy came by while Jennings was getting dressed for the school board meeting in Jewell Hill. Jennings felt more tolerant of the boy now that he and Roma were getting along again. So when Buddy stomped up on the porch and called out, Jennings felt a warmth for the boy, because now Buddy and Roma were associated in his mind. Jennings recalled what Roma had said last night when he'd asked her again if she'd been mad at him for leaving in a huff and staying gone those two weeks. "Not mad," she'd said. "Disappointed." And then she'd said: "But I know how to keep a relationship up on blocks till weeds grow up around it if I have to."

Jennings stood in the open door with a tie draped around his turned up shirt collar. "What say, Henry." He motioned Buddy in and finished tying his tie.

"You know what?" Buddy said. "There's this mall opening over in Jewell Hill, and they've got this whale in a big tank out in the parking lot. On a flatbed truck—that's what it said on WWJH. You know that?"

"I do now, Henry."

"Let's go see that thing!"

"I'm going to Jewell Hill but I won't have time to see any whale. Got to go to that meeting this evening."

"Which meeting?"

"Why, the school board meeting. See if I can help Lloyd Sutherland and his bunch keep the board from closing The Kingdom School.—What did you think we were talking about for two hours over there in The Kingdom the other night?"

"I don't know. Thought you all were just talking."

"Henry, Henry," Jennings said, shaking his head. "You want to go with me to that meeting? Roma's gonna be there, and Edna Rae. Didn't she mention it?"

"I want to see that whale," Buddy said. "We could go early, see the whale first."

"Good Lord, a whale!" Jennings said. "Didn't you fetch my mail. Go fetch my mail before I have to go."

"Can I drive the truck?"

"You can be down to the box and back before you get that truck started and turned around."

"It's not good for that truck to just set, the way it does."

"Well, take it, then, and bring me my mail."

Buddy was out of the house and down the steps in a flash. Jennings heard the old pickup start, whip around at the edge of the yard, and head down the drive to the mailbox. By the time he'd put on his jacket, gathered together some papers, and stepped outside to his worktable under the sycamores in the yard, Buddy had returned with a bundle of magazines, newspapers, and envelopes.

Jennings sat at the worktable going through the mail. He

picked out two business-size envelopes, held them up to the sky, then opened them and removed checks, which he dropped in his inside jacket pocket.

"How much?" Buddy asked.

"Not nearly enough," Jennings said. He scooped up the mail, climbed the porch steps, dropped it all into a tomato basket, and set the basket inside the door. "Let's go, if you're going with me to Jewell Hill. I want to stop at The Trading Post on the way in."

"Won't be anybody at that school board meeting, anyway," Buddy said, as he followed Jennings to his Skyhawk. "They'll all be out there to see that whale."

"You're probably right about that, Henry," Jennings said, sliding under the wheel.

Jennings drove down the Newfound Road and slowed to cross the first one-lane bridge. Just beyond the bridge, as he was picking up speed again on a straight stretch that ran alongside the creek, he saw in his rear view mirror an old brown car pull out onto the road behind him. He hadn't noticed it as he'd come down off the bridge. Now the car was coming up behind him, coming up fast.

"Who's that?" Jennings asked Buddy.

Buddy turned in his seat and looked back. "Uh-oh."

"Uh-oh, what?"

"You know who that is?—That's Cecil Pedigo's old brown Pontiac."

Jennings watched the car in the side mirror. It came up on his bumper with a roar. "Well, damn, Cecil!" Jennings said. He tapped his brake—to back Cecil off. The bumpers banged together. Then Cecil swung into the left lane and started past

Jennings. Jennings sped up and eased over into the center of the straight road.

"It's Cecil all right. I see his old deputy sheriff's cap," Buddy said. "He's trying to run us off the road."

"If I let him get up beside me, he'll do it, too," Jennings said, and accelerated again.

Still, Cecil kept coming. Jennings could hear the deep-throated sound of the Pontiac's engine, straining. The front end of the Pontiac was easing up on the left, even with Jennings' left rear wheel. Jennings pressed the accelerator to the floor and glanced at the speedometer. Seventy. Seventy-five.

"Don't let him git up beside you, Jennings," Buddy shouted.

Jennings whipped into the left lane, slowed to sixty, and took a long turn, then headed into another straight stretch that ran along the creek. Off the right-hand side of the road was a long slope down to the creek,—and no guard-rail. God amighty! If Cecil got up beside him anywhere along here, he could push him right off over the bank and down into Newfound Creek. He shot forward and whipped completely over into the left lane. He heard Cecil's Pontiac growl and in the rear view saw it switch back into the right lane. He was trying to pass on the right now!—Well, he wouldn't! Damn fool! What was he up to?

Jennings whipped back into the right lane, tapped his brakes, then whipped to the left again, and when Cecil's Pontiac followed, tapped his brakes again. He went down the Newfound Road whipping from left to right, right to left, made it to the second one-lane bridge ahead of Cecil and bounded across it, taking to the air as he came down on the other side.

As he righted the Skyhawk he glanced back in the mirror, hoping Cecil had missed the bridge and gone into the creek. But he saw the grill of the Pontiac ride up over the bridge and come crashing down onto the road. But he made it to the stop sign at the end of the Newfound Road, and since he could see both ways, whipped right onto 1533 and headed for The Trading Post. Cecil held off, followed him at a distance. Jennings slid into the parking lot at The Trading Post, gravel flying up under the Skyhawk. "You stay right with me," he told Buddy, as he flung open the door, and, pocketing his keys, walked toward The Trading Post. "Don't look back," he told Buddy. "Just keep walking."

"It's Hilliard," Buddy whispered. "It's Hilliard, you know it?"

"What do you mean—Hilliard?"

"Hilliard's sicced Cecil on you, because of the school board thing, I bet money."

"How do you know so much about it? Awhile ago you didn't even know there was a school board meeting."

"I know more'n I let on sometimes," Buddy said. "I remember what Lloyd Sutherland said over in The Kingdom the other night. He said Cecil's Hilliard's bulldog."

"We'll see," Jennings said.

He walked up to the loafers bench by the front door of The Trading Post, where Delano Crumm, Wiley Woolford, and Dee Rhodommer were sitting. Delano was in the middle of a story. "So then, after you've baked your carp, on that pine board, with them bacon strips acrosst him, so that bacon grease soaks all the way down through that carp and into your pine board,—what you do is, you eat the board and throw the carp away!" Delano Crumm looked up at Jennings. "Ain't that right, Jennings? You've heard that. You bake a carp on a pine board, with strips of bacon, then eat the board and throw the carp away!"

"That's right, Delano, I've heard it," Jennings said. "How are you fellers?" Jennings glanced casually toward the gravel lot and saw that Cecil's brown Pontiac had pulled into the lot, and Cecil was getting out of his car.

173

"About as well as common, Jennings," Delano said.

"How're you, little Shelton?" Wiley Woodford said. "Getting over that yaller janders?"

"I'm ok," Buddy said.

"Here comes Deputy Dawg," Delano Crumm said.

Jennings glanced toward the parking lot and saw Cecil approaching.

"With that beeper still," Dee Rhodommer said.

"And that deputy sheriff hat," Wiley Woolford said. "Old Cecil, what you'd call all hat and no cattle." Wiley lowered his head, and as Cecil shuffled up, making a noise in the gravel with his shoes, Wiley looked up again. "Been catching any carp lately, Cecil? Delano here's got a good recipe for you, if you have."

Jennings watched out of the corner of his eye as Cecil tugged at the bill of his deputy hat and shifted his weight to one foot. "I've not been fishing lately," Cecil said. With a hiss, Cecil spit between his wide-spaced front teeth onto the ground.

Jennings had thought about Cecil from time to time since he'd spoken to him in Hilliard's office. He remembered how he'd caught Cecil red-handed once years ago stealing muskrats and mink from Jennings' traps on Newfound Creek. And Cecil's pea-brained braggadocio about killing the last squirrel in Cordell County riled Jennings even in the recollection of it. "Let me ask you something Cecil," Jennings said. "Where'd you learn to drive?"

Cecil stared at Jennings with flat, expressionless gray-green eyes, but said nothing.

"I ask because I don't think you've learned yet, have you?"

Again, Cecil said nothing. Delano, Wiley, and Dee looked at one another, and lowered their heads. Dee became suddenly intent on cutting a notch in the loafers bench with his pocket-knife. Jennings nudged Buddy with his elbow, turned, and walked toward the horseshoe pits at the far end of The Trading Post. Buddy walked close beside him.

"If he comes out here, then what?" Buddy muttered.

"We'll see," Jennings said, and picked up all four horseshoes from the pit and handed two to Buddy. "Pitch to the other stob," he told Buddy.

Jennings stood while Buddy stepped down into the pit and pitched first one, then the other horseshoe to the opposite pit. Then he stepped into the pit and pitched his two.

"First time I ever saw anybody pitch horseshoes in a suit, with a tie on," Buddy said.

Jennings pitched. The first shoe landed with a clank on top of one of Buddy's, and bounced out of the pit. The second turned up against the stob and rested there. "Leaner," he said to Buddy.

They walked together to the opposite pit. Jennings figured that when he picked up his horseshoes and turned back, he'd see where Cecil was. He turned and looked up. Cecil had followed. He'd come to the end of the building, was standing there watching them. Jennings pitched back to the pit closest to Cecil; then Buddy pitched. As they walked back to the first pit, Cecil stepped toward it too.

"Something I can do for you, Cecil?" Jennings said, picking up his shoes.

"These here articles," Cecil said. "These articles you've been putting in the paper about the schools."

Jennings stepped into the pit, and, turning his back on Cecil, leveled a horseshoe at the iron post in the opposite pit. It probably wasn't a good idea to turn your back on Cecil, but he'd be damned if he'd let Cecil think he was afraid of him. "Why, I didn't know you took any interest in education, Cecil." He pitched his first shoe. "What has education ever done for you, Cec—?" He was about to pitch the second shoe when he heard the swarp of Cecil's trousers behind him,—right, he shouldn't have turned—and before he could turn was stunned by a blow to the back of the head. Everything went black around him, stars exploded inside his skull, and suddenly he felt sick.

When he could see again he was down in the horseshoe pit, on one knee, weaving, about to pitch over, and Cecil was coming at him with something in his hand. He lunged forward, hit Cecil in the crotch with his head, and as Cecil fell backwards, he came down on top of him, reaching for whatever Cecil had in his hand. He looked toward Cecil's hand, lying on top of Cecil, and saw Buddy's foot stomping the hand. Stomping, over and over. Until he stomped a blackjack from Cecil's hand and kicked it out of the way.

Grunting and cursing, Cecil rolled from under him. Jennings scrambled after him, grabbing onto Cecil's shirt, then his pants leg. He was getting away until Buddy hit him in the side of the head with a horseshoe. Cecil's legs went limp. Jennings grabbed his right foot and held on. Buddy drew back to hit him again in the head with the horseshoe. "No, don't," Jennings said. He drew himself up, first onto one knee, and, steadying himself with his hand, stood. He felt the back of his head; it was warm and sticky. He brought away blood on his fingers. He held up his hand to Buddy. "No, don't hit him again." Weaving a little, he looked down at Cecil. "Damn you, Cecil, get up. I said get up."

He stood watching as Cecil rolled over, got up on one knee.

Jennings reached him a hand and pulled him to his feet. Cecil's beeper had come off his belt as he rolled and lay on the ground at some distance. Jennings motioned to the beeper, then to Buddy. Buddy fetched the beeper and gave it to Cecil.

"My blackjack," Cecil said. He picked his deputy hat off the ground.

Jennings saw that the burr of Cecil's ear, where Buddy had hit him with the horseshoe, was bloody. "You're not getting your damned blackjack," Jennings told him. He spotted the blackjack on the ground where Buddy had kicked it and went over to pick it up. As he bent down, he sickened and his head swam. He straightened and motioned for Buddy to pick it up. "Get outta here, Cecil," he said. "You're not getting your damned blackjack."

Buddy came and stood by him. He watched as Cecil shuffled off behind The Trading Post, first holding his beeper in his hand, then making repeated efforts to hook it on his belt. He never succeeded. Cecil continued on behind The Trading Post, disappeared from view for a minute, and then came out in the edge of the parking lot. He got in his Pontiac. Sat there a minute. Probably trying to find his keys. The old Pontiac started and Cecil left the lot.

"Told you," Buddy said. "He aimed to scare you away from that school board meeting."

"Well, he played hob."

"You going anyway? Your head's cut. You're bleeding like a stuck hog. Your coat's tore."

"Nothing that can't be fixed," Jennings said. And he always had a change of clothes in the car. Jennings muttered to himself. He'd been ready to leave this place, but he'd be damned if he was going to be *run off*.

"Let's go around this way," Buddy said.

"Hell, no," Jennings said. "I want them to see me. Delano and Wiley. And Dee Rhodommer."

Buddy following, Jennings walked past the front of The Trading Post, back past the loafers on the bench. "Boys," he said.

Delano, Wiley, and Dee looked up in astonishment. "You all right, Jennings?"

Jennings stood there realizing he was bloody, his jacket torn, his gray trousers covered with red clay. "I'm fine, boys."

"You sure, Jennings?" Delano asked.

"I'm all right."

Dee Rhodommer stepped forward and fingered the blackjack Jennings was still holding. "Cecil's head whacker," Dee said. He took it from Jennings' hand and tapped the side of his own head—gently—as if testing the blackjack. Dee's eyes rolled; he made a circle with his mouth.

"I tell you, things is picking up around here," Wiley Woolford said.

"Happening, seems like, fastern they used to," Dee said, handing the blackjack back to Jennings.

"If this comes to court," Wiley said, "I reckon we're witnesses."

"It won't come to court," Jennings said. "I won't be bringing it to court, and I don't think Cecil will!"

"Goes to show you, though," Delano said. "You set in one place long enough, you'll see something!"

"If you fellers come to that school board meeting this evening, you may see something else!" Jennings said.

"You going to the meeting," Delano said, "hurt like you are?"

"I aim to be there," Jennings said.

178

He left them sitting there astonished, looking at one another, walked on to the Skyhawk and got in.

Buddy got in on the other side, slammed the door, and scooted down in the seat. "I'm keeping Cecil's blackjack," Buddy said.

Jennings started the Skyhawk and reached over. "Give it here," he said, and pulled out onto the road.

23

He was by-god determined to make it to the school board meeting on time—and did.

"There's Roma—she's waiting for you," Buddy said, as he pulled Jennings' Skyhawk into the lot beside the school board building in Jewell Hill. Jennings had let Buddy drive after stopping to get his head patched up, and after he'd taken two Tylenol for the pain.

Roma was standing outside the school board office with Edna Rae. Jennings got out carefully, so as not to bump his head, and walked toward them. He could see Roma's eyes widen when she saw his head was bandaged.

"Jennings? What on earth?"

"Why, honey, you look like you've been sacking wildcats," Edna Rae said.

"Thanks for coming, Roma," Jennings said. "Edna Rae," he said, nodding to his cousin, then flinching from the pain. He thought of a doll's head—one of those that, if you tipped it one way, its eyes closed. Only his head felt as if there were something loose inside, rolling around in the back of his head.

"Jennings, what happened?" Roma asked.

"Been in a fight, that's what!" Buddy said, as he walked up.

Jennings took the car keys out of Buddy's hand and pocketed them.

"Fight?" Roma said. "How did you . . . . ?"

"See, they've got this whale in a big tank in the parking lot out at the mall," Buddy said.

"Whale?" Roma said. "What's that got to do . . . . ?"

"Nothing!" Jennings said.

Roma took him by the arm, walked him to the side of the building—away from the entrance—where she inspected the bandage on the back of his head. She touched the bandage gently. "And you've come to this meeting anyway—hurt and bandaged up?"

"I'll be all right," Jennings said. "I was looking for Lloyd Sutherland—to tell him I *wasn't* coming to this meeting. Then Cecil Pedigo jumped me. I changed my mind. I'm not about to be run off."

"But this bandage—where—?"

"Dick Lovell put it on," Buddy said.

"The veterinarian?" Edna Rae said.

"After the fight," Buddy said, "we left The Trading Post and headed on over into The Kingdom . . . looking for Lloyd Sutherland. Come up on Dick Lovell's van. He'd been somewhere doctoring cows."

"The back of my head was bleeding," Jennings said. "I could feel it was laid open."

"So Jennings flagged Dick Lovell down and got bandaged up," Buddy said.

Jennings grinned. "Lovell didn't want to do it. Said he wasn't a doctor. Said he was a large animal veterinarian. I said, well, hell, I'm a large animal."

"He fixed Jennings up right there on the side of the road," Buddy said.

"You know what Lovell was afraid of?" Jennings said. "Malpractice! He said, 'If you tell anybody I patched you up, I'll deny it!'"

"We never did get to see that whale," Buddy said.

Jennings touched the back of his head. "I wished you'd hush about that damned whale!"

Jennings kept waiting for Lloyd Sutherland to show up. It turned out that Lloyd was already inside, with Hilliard Shelton, Thurman Venable, the school superintendent, and other members of the board. Lloyd had already talked to Hilliard, who opened the meeting by saying that Mr. Jennings Wells would make a statement on behalf of residents of The Kingdom community.

From the back row, Edna Rae, raising her hand like a schoolchild, corrected Hilliard: "That's *Dr.* Wells."

Hilliard rapped his gavel, then shrugged. "All right. *Dr.* Wells."

Standing at the front of the room with Lloyd Sutherland, Jennings winked at Roma. He stood looking over the gathering, surprised to see Wiley Woolford, Delano Crumm, and Dee Rhodommer there. And lots of other people who probably had never attended a school board meeting in their entire lives.

"Well, go ahead, *Dr.* Wells," Hilliard said.

Jennings turned, startled. He remembered how he used to be caught off guard years ago, when Miss Duckett, his third grade teacher, would have him stand at the front of the room during silent reading sessions and answer questions for other students who raised their hands. And often he'd be staring out the window, paying no attention, while two or three students had their hands up for help.

He tried to collect his thoughts and launched into an opening statement. He wanted it known that it was wrong, first of all, to think that mountain people didn't value education. They did. (He noticed Buddy whispering to Roma in the back of the room.) People wanted better schools, schools that served their communities. But a bigger school was not automatically a better school.

A bigger school wasn't automatically worse, either, Hilliard observed.

No, Jennings allowed. But it was interesting that if you looked around the world nowadays, you saw people everywhere rejecting collectivization and here we were still collectivizing our schools!

Hilliard didn't see Jennings' point. Of course not, Jennings thought. Hilliard's mind wouldn't leap. He didn't respond to Hilliard. Instead, he moved on: our young people didn't learn the history of their own place, yet it was clear that the more we knew about our own place, the more we were apt to care about it, and to want to take care of it. But that history was ignored or obscured. Bankers and industrialists had named mountain towns after themselves, as if our communities hadn't had names already. If you looked underneath these names on the maps and roadsigns, you'd find the old names, given by the settlers. Underneath Barton—Spring Creek; under van den Berg—Red Oak; under McEwing—Pick Britches. These industrialists had robbed the region not only of its mineral wealth, but even of its names. And thus of memory and a sense of the past.

Hilliard sat, gavel in hand, shaking his head. He still didn't see Jennings' point.

Jennings explained: this proposal to close The Kingdom School was just one more step in a process, a process of collectivization that weakened local communities, ignored and obscured history.—And as he said it he knew this wasn't going over, wasn't going over at all, not even with the folks he was supposed to be representing.

With the faintest hint of a smirk, Hilliard Shelton wanted to know if *Dr.* Wells had any children in attendance at The Kingdom School.

No, he didn't.

Had *Dr.* Wells ever had any children in attendance at The Kingdom School?

No, he hadn't.

Then what was *Dr.* Wells' interest in The Kingdom School?

The board was well aware of his interest, Jennings said. He was representing people who did have children attending The Kingdom School, families who had been sending their children there for generations. Jennings had attended The Kingdom School himself.

Was *Dr.* Wells a lawyer? Hilliard wanted to know.

Jennings wished Edna Rae hadn't brought up the doctor business. "Hilliard," he said, "just call me Jennings. You know I'm not a lawyer." He turned to the gathering. "Look, we all know one another here; we know why we're here. I'd like to talk about that."

Roma and Edna Rae clapped approval; then everyone else applauded and began speaking to one another. Jennings felt as if he'd finally scored a point.

Hilliard was asking questions for the record, he said. It was important what the record showed. He hoped Jennings agreed.

Jennings did agree. Jennings also wanted the record to show that any taxpayer had a legitimate interest in the county's schools, whether he had children enrolled in the schools or not. Did Hilliard agree with that? Hilliard did. Jennings also wanted the record to show that you didn't have to be a lawyer to take an interest in school matters, or to represent a group of parents in a matter involving their children's school. Did Hilliard agree with that?

Hilliard didn't believe anybody said you had to be a lawyer. . . .

But Hilliard had implied that, Jennings said. So, did Hilliard agree that you didn't have to be a lawyer to represent one side of an issue in a school board hearing?

Hilliard agreed and he was glad to see Jennings agreed that there were two sides to this issue.

Jennings turned to the audience. "We're in such agreement here, why don't we just shake hands around and go home?"

Again the audience applauded. Another point!

Hilliard rapped his gavel and called the group to order. It appeared, he said, that Jennings had been in an accident. It appeared that Jennings was in some pain. He wondered if Jennings felt up to continuing.

A chair scooted back noisily. Jennings looked around to see Lloyd Sutherland, angered by Hilliard's ploy, come up from his chair. His nephew Bobby pulled Lloyd back down into his chair.

Jennings held out his hand toward Lloyd, to reassure him. "Appearances can be so misleading! Can't they, Hilliard? I may *appear* to have been in an accident, but I think you know"— and he touched the bandage on the back of his head—"I think you know this was no accident. I may *appear* to be in pain. But I've never felt better. I certainly do want to continue!"

Hilliard didn't know that anything more needed to be said.

The issue was clear-cut: did they keep The Kingdom School open, or close it? Did they stand still educationally in Cordell County, or go forward, progressively, by consolidating the old Kingdom School with a modern, up-to-date, state-of-the-art educational plant?

Suddenly, to his amazement, Jennings saw Roma stand at the back of the room and raise her hand for permission to speak.

Hilliard was startled too, Jennings could tell. "Yes?" Hilliard said.

Roma tossed her head and pushed her hair back with her right hand. "I think there's a lot more to be said!"

Jennings saw Delano Crumm nod sagely. The audience murmured affirmatively.

Edna Rae rose and stood beside Roma. "I went to that meeting about the landfill," Edna Rae said. "And everybody there had a chance to speak. Everybody got three minutes. I think everybody that wants to ought to have a chance to speak!" Edna Rae sat down quickly.

Hilliard's brow wrinkled. He pushed his glasses up onto his forehead and rubbed the sides of his nose between thumb and forefinger. "Well, you're talking!"

Roma nudged Edna Rae. Jennings could see Edna Rae hadn't expected to say anything else. Edna Rae rose again, hesitantly, and stood there.

"You wanted a chance to speak," Hilliard said. "So speak."

"Well . . ." Edna Rae looked around the room. Well, Edna Rae just believed The Kingdom School was a good school. People who'd gone to The Kingdom School, they'd done right well. There'd been doctors and lawyers and judges, and she could name them, that'd gone to The Kingdom School. And it'd always been more than a school. She remembered they'd had war bond rallies at the school back during the war. People would put on a program, pick and sing, have a good time, and then buy war bonds!—Jennings thought Edna Rae was going to continue but she sat down suddenly.

There was an awkward silence. Jennings glanced over at Hilliard.

"I been studying on something," Lloyd Sutherland said, rising from his chair. "They say it'd be better for our younguns to consolidate because they've got computers at that other school. They say the children can be hauled now that we've got the roads. Well, how come roads is just one way—to haul *out* to the big school? Why can't we haul computers *in*, over into The Kingdom? How come it's always a road out but never a road in?"

How about that? Jennings thought. Lloyd proved something he'd hoped was right: if people would just do it, they could argue the issues that concerned them better than someone could argue for them.

Hilliard didn't see that the meeting was getting anywhere, though. He doubted there'd be time to let everybody speak. It just wasn't a practical way to. . . .

"I want to say something!" Suddenly, Buddy was on his feet. He'd been whispering to Roma since the start of the meeting. Jennings had noticed Roma, two or three times, trying to shush him. ". . . about Cordell County High School," Buddy continued. He looked round. "I'm the only one here that's ever gone there. I went a year and a half, and I quit it! I won't ever go back, either. One bunch over there just thinks about football and basketball. . . ."

Jennings stood to the side watching Roma as her head turned quickly from Buddy to Edna Rae to him. Her face shone with delight and pleasure at the turn the meeting had taken.

". . . and the other bunch smokes dope."

"I've heard it's the truth!" Edna Rae said.

187

"The mothers of some of the cheerleaders run the school!" Buddy said. "And grades don't make any difference. You can get these blank report cards and just fill 'em out! Excuse slips, too. You can't go down the hall hardly without getting into a fight. Half the girls are going to have babies."

"It didn't used to be that way," Edna Rae said.

"One ninth grader, when I was still going there, was meeting her boyfriend out in the parking lot," Buddy said. "He had been in the penitentiary. And one teacher come to school with a black eye her boyfriend gave her. Another teacher was dating a student. You might as well not leave anything in your locker; you couldn't lock it. And Jennings has got as many books at his house as there are in the Cordell County School library."

"Jennings always was good in his books," Edna Rae said. She was bolder now about speaking out of turn, Jennings noticed. She wasn't bothering now to raise her hand!

"Cordell's not a school, not like The Kingdom School. I know," Buddy said. "I've been to both."

Lloyd Sutherland stepped in front of Hilliard and Thurman Venable, the superintendent. "We don't want to send younguns into a mess like that!" he said. "What we ought to be talking about is fixing Cordell County School before we think about doing away with The Kingdom School!"

To Jennings' astonishment, he watched as Delano Crumm rose to speak, although Hilliard was rapping with his gavel. "You know," Delano said, "I hadn't thought about it till Lloyd mentioned it, but he's right: a road goes in the same as it goes out. Ain't that right, Wiley?"

Wiley Woolford stood. "That's right. The roads is good now, but still, in a bus, it's a good hour's ride, hour and a half, maybe, one way, from over in The Kingdom. Now, that's hard on little kids."

Suddenly everyone was standing, talking to one another! Beautiful! Jennings thought.

"Mr. Chairman! Mr. Chairman!" Edna Rae was calling.

Jennings stepped past the rows of chairs to Roma's side. "Fox on the run, Jennings!" Roma said. "Fox on the run!"

Hilliard was rapping with his gavel. "We'll carry this meeting over!" he said.

"Till when?" Roma called.

"I don't know. We'll set a date and announce it."

"Be sure you do let us know," Edna Rae said. "Because we'll all want to come!"

"This meeting is adjourned!" Hilliard said.

But Jennings doubted if more than two or three people heard him. They were all talking to one another.

24

After the school board meeting they stood out in the parking lot—Jennings, Roma, Edna Rae and Buddy—arguing about whether they should all go to Roma's or Jennings' house. It didn't make any difference to Edna Rae, either place was fine, but she thought maybe she ought to get on home, Aunt Velma might call. Edna Rae was excited and chattery, the way she'd been the afternoon they'd driven to Johnson City to the Conway Twitty concert. She worried about Aunt Velma. Aunt Velma, she'd never been further than Lexington in her life when she up and went with her church group to New York City. Saw all the street people. Didn't have any manners at all, Aunt Velma said. Never was as glad to be back home in her life. Edna Rae worried about Aunt Velma because she wouldn't take her medicine like she was supposed to. She saved it, so it would last longer. Edna Rae wanted Roma to talk to her, because Aunt Velma wouldn't listen to Edna Rae. Roma promised she would.—Edna Rae felt so sorry for her, she was so old and feeble, but Aunt Velma would drive you crazy if you let her. Like, the other night she'd wanted to watch Billy Graham on tv but her picture went out. So she called Edna Rae wanting Edna Rae to turn the program on and tell it to her over the phone.

Jennings shifted his weight from one foot to the other while Edna Rae rattled on. His head was beginning to throb. He needed another Tylenol. Something. A drink, maybe. He wondered if they were going to stand there all night.

By pleading pain and his bandaged head, and reminding Edna Rae that she could call Aunt Velma and check on her— she didn't have to sit at home waiting for Aunt Velma to call her—Jennings succeeded in getting Edna Rae and Roma to come by his house. He let Buddy drive the Skyhawk and rode home with his eyes closed most of the way.

At the house Edna Rae got out of Roma's Mercury still talking! In the house Jennings had to interrupt her to remind her to call Aunt Velma. She came back from the telephone— Aunt Velma was all right—and reported the entire conversation while Jennings made drinks—two good stiff ones for him and Roma (the drink was his own invention; he called it a Running Jack after a local character). All Edna Rae wanted was just a little of Buddy's Coke.

Edna Rae tickled Jennings. She didn't know when she'd had so much fun! That meeting had got her all stirred up, got her to remembering so many things. Did Jennings remember the time when they were gathering walnuts with Grandma Wells over there by The Kingdom School and all the butterflies lit on them?

How could he ever forget it?

"Butterflies?" Roma said.

Yes! Edna Rae guessed there'd been five hundred big orange

and black butterflies. More like a thousand! They were sitting there resting and all of a sudden these butterflies just came down out of the air and lit all over them—her and Jennings, just a little boy then, and Grandma Wells.

It sounded unbelievable, Jennings admitted as he served the drinks. But he remembered it just the way Edna Rae told it. He winked at Roma. "Things like that happen. A fellow told me he saw five hundred redbirds on a branch bank once." He'd told Roma that story.

And did Jennings remember how Grandma Wells had whispered to them? Don't move, she said. Don't move. But after a while Edna Rae had moved, and all the butterflies flew off again. Grandma Wells had said it was a sign.

A sign of what? Roma wanted to know.

Grandma Wells never said what it was a sign of, Edna Rae remembered. But she'd said it was a sign!

It was a sign monarch butterflies were migrating, that's what it was a sign of, Jennings allowed. He wondered what would happen if he took a Tylenol with a Running Jack.

Anyway, Edna Rae was so proud of Jennings for getting Hilliard Shelton to put off closing the school.

Jennings didn't think he deserved any credit for that. He'd been blundering around up there until Roma and Edna Rae broke the whole thing open. He'd felt about as useless as—well, he wouldn't say.

Edna Rae admitted that Jennings had been talking over people's heads a little. She never knew half the time what Jennings was talking about, but she knew he did. And even if she didn't know what he was talking about, Jennings sounded so good, she could just listen! Jennings had got people to thinking. What Lloyd Sutherland said, that was good. Even Delano

Crumm spoke up, and Wiley Woolford. And most of the time all they did was sit and listen, like bumps on a log.

But it was Edna Rae and Roma who got everybody to talking, Jennings insisted.

Didn't Roma do good? Edna Rae patted the back of Roma's hand. Edna Rae wouldn't have had the nerve to stand up and talk in that meeting if Roma hadn't stood up and talked first.

Jennings winked at Roma. Roma had nerve, for sure, Jennings said. How many times had he said to her, You've got a lot of nerve!

Roma smiled.

Still, they hadn't really won anything, Jennings cautioned. All they'd done was buy a little time.

Edna Rae knew that, but she felt like celebrating anyway. Maybe Jennings could make her just a wee tiny drink, just a. . . .

Jennings made her a weak, watery, pitiful drink. Not a Running Jack, more nearly a Limping Jack.

Maybe they had just bought time, Edna Rae conceded. But every time the school business came up, they'd all be right there, and they'd talk Hilliard's ears off! Jennings could put things in the paper about it, more and more people would get interested. Lord, she couldn't wait till the next meeting! Buddy would have to go, too, and tell about that mess at Cordell County High.

Buddy did fine, Jennings agreed. He gave Buddy a pat on the back. That took nerve, too—getting up there in front of his Uncle Hilliard like that.

Buddy said he despised Hilliard and wished Hilliard wasn't his uncle.

Jennings didn't doubt that the school was as bad as Buddy had said it was. Nevertheless, Buddy ought to be in school.

Now, Jennings, don't start! Roma said.

Buddy wasn't hurting Hilliard by not going to school, Jennings said. He was only hurting himself. Right now, the way Jennings figured it, Buddy was like a hog under an apple tree, eating, sleeping, and never looking up to see where the food was coming from.

Would Jennings hush? Roma wanted to know. Buddy had been sick; he was still taking medicine.

Jennings knew Buddy had been sick. He was getting better now. When he got well, then what? Buddy reckoned he'd be free, did he? Like his Grandpa Shelton, who always said he liked to be free. Well, Buddy's grandpa hadn't been all that free. And Buddy couldn't expect to be both free and ignorant.—But let's say Buddy got well, let's say he was free—then what? He'd get him a job, yeah, live some place, but not at Hilliard's. OK. Let's say Buddy was free, had him a job, a roof over his head, clothes, enough to eat. Then what?

That sounded all right to Buddy!

Sure it did. But after all that, the then-what? days came, on and on. Henry had to consider the then-what? days. He'd be beating around in a pickup with a baseball cap on top of a half bushel of hair. Then his hair would start to recede, he'd round out from drinking beer, so in his sleeveless padded jacket he'd begin to look like a walking hand grenade. By that time some girl would have struck his fancy and he'd have her set up in a doublewide. Then what? He'd wake up some day and look back, and wouldn't know how it had all happened. Then what?

How did Jennings know so much about everything? Buddy wanted to know.

Just look around, Jennings suggested. All he was talking about was what Buddy, or anybody else who looked, could see everywhere.

194

Roma wanted both of them just to hush. Honestly! Jennings went off without a word. Nobody knew where he was for two weeks. Then he came traipsing back and jumped down a sick boy's throat!

Edna Rae thought Roma ought to hush, too. She could tell them all why they were arguing—because they cared about one another.

Edna Rae was right, Jennings allowed; he did care what happened to Buddy, and he just hated to see. . . . He watched as Buddy took a small black notebook from his hip pocket. The boy looked to Roma, Jennings thought, as if asking permission. Roma glanced at Jennings, then back at Buddy, and nodded approval.

What was this? Jennings wanted to know, taking the notebook Buddy held out to him.

Well, maybe Buddy knew more than Jennings thought. For instance, Buddy had been writing a book, just the way Jennings wrote books. He'd been working on it ever since he got sick. Actually, since before he got sick. But it wasn't till he lay sick all that time over at Roma's while Jennings was off and gone, that he'd read all the books that Jennings had written. Buddy had read about how Jennings and his mother played and sang at the Rocky Top Festival, how they'd gone together back then. Buddy had put it all together, figured it out, the way that man over in Granger County had found out who ran over his daddy by writing everything down in a notebook.

Jennings leafed through the notebook. Yeah, Buddy had told him about all that. He remembered. And he knew Buddy must have heard talk. But that's all it was—talk. He'd loved Buddy's mother. He'd wanted to marry her—back then. He'd wanted her to stay in Cordell County and marry him. But Buddy's mother had a mind to leave.

Jennings scanned quickly to the end of the notebook, read the last page. He got up, stepped over to a bookcase, and pulled out a battered copy of *How America Came to Cordell County*. The book was held together by rubber bands. The copy he read from, he'd carried it about in cars for years, and more than once it had been left out in the rain! He removed the rubber bands and flipped to a center section of photographs. Pointing to one, he asked Buddy who that was.

That was his Mama, Buddy said, and he added that Roma's copy of *How America Came to Cordell County* was in a lot better shape than Jennings'.

Jennings didn't doubt that. And that fellow beside Buddy's Mama, who was that?

That was Jennings, playing a guitar.

Right. And that fellow could have been Buddy's daddy. Would have been. But wasn't. Something Jennings had never told Buddy: he'd seen Buddy once, when Buddy was about six months old. Up in Ohio. He'd gone there after he'd found out where Buddy's mother was, to get her to come home. Come home and marry him. She wouldn't. Sorry, son, but he wasn't Buddy's daddy.

Buddy sat holding the notebook Jennings returned to him. Shoot! He'd thought he had it figured. If Jennings wasn't, then who was?

Why, Jennings thought there wasn't much doubt that Buddy's father was Jack Daugherty, a country musician Buddy's mother had joined up with after she left Cordell County. Daugherty had been killed in a car crash in Baton Rouge, Louisiana. Buddy's mother had been in the accident, too. And so had Buddy, for that matter! Only he hadn't been born yet!—Hadn't his mother ever talked to him about his father?

Buddy just barely remembered his mother, and she didn't

ever come home, or even write. He didn't think Grandma Shelton knew anything about his daddy. When he used to ask her, Grandma Shelton never would tell him anything. She'd just think of something for him to do.

Well, Buddy was a big boy now, and he ought to try to get in touch with his mother and talk to her. In the meantime, Jennings had just thought of something for Buddy to do: he could take the flashlight and go outside and see if Jennings had been right about that tire. When they were coming up the drive earlier, he thought he felt the right front tire going down.

After he had gone outside with Jennings' big six-cell flashlight, Roma wished again that Jennings wouldn't jump all over Buddy about school. Edna Rae agreed. Jennings shouldn't be like the woman with the sick cat. Surely Jennings had heard about the woman with the sick cat. She had to give it medicine every day and every day she had the awfullest time getting the cat to take that medicine. The fur flew! Then one day she knocked the medicine over and it spilled out on the floor. The cat walked over and licked it up.—OK. Jennings would remember that—the woman with the sick cat. Edna Rae. She never failed to tickle Jennings.

He heard Buddy pound in on the porch. The door swung open, the beam of the big flashlight cut across Jennings' face before Buddy turned it off and stood in front of them, a look of incredulity on his face. He brushed his hair out of his right eye with the back of his hand. "Three tires! Three!" he said. "Flat as biscuits. You were right, Jennings. And look here. I pulled this out of the left front with the wire pliers in your glove compartment."

He handed Jennings a bristling metal object Jennings recognized at once. Uh-oh. As they were coming up the drive earlier and he'd felt the right front tire going soft, the thought had crossed his mind that he might have picked up one of these devilish devices, and if so, the right front tire wouldn't be the only one going down.

"What is that thing?" Roma asked.

"Why, it's a jackrock," Edna Rae said. "At least they call them jackrocks. There was a picture of one in the paper during the last strike."

"You take a piece of metal," Jennings explained, turning the jackrock in his hand, "say, a twenty penny nail, anything sharp, twist it up into a curlicue." He dropped it on the table, picked it up, dropped it again. "See, any way it falls, a sharp point sticks up. Sow a bunch of these on a road, you can ruin a lot of tires."

"During that last strike," Edna Rae said, the miners put them on fishing rods and cast 'em down off the road bank. If their people come up the road in cars, they'd reel them in. If the scabs come up the road, they left them laying!"

"You were coming along right behind us," Jennings said to Roma. "You probably picked some up too."

"No, her tires are all right," Buddy said. "I checked 'em good."

"I'll bet, though, there's still some of them in the drive," Jennings said, "between the house and the mailbox."

Buddy volunteered to take the flashlight and go look for more jackrocks in the long drive between the house and the road, but Jennings said no and took the flashlight. He suspected he knew what this meant. So did Buddy. He bet it was Cecil Pedigo who strowed the jackrocks. He'd seen Cecil down at The Trading Post one day rolling a jackrock around in his hand, tossing it up and catching it. Cecil strowed the jackrocks.—Strew, Jennings said. But yes, Buddy was probably right, Cecil probably had scattered them.

Jennings went to the window and stood looking down in the direction of the barn, the branch bank, and the road beyond. It was hard to see out because of the glare of lamplight on the panes. He cupped his hands over his eyes to cut out the glare. Had Cecil come up here after their run-in at The Trading Post? He hadn't seen Cecil skulking around anywhere at the school board meeting. Jennings wondered if maybe. . . . Behind him he heard Edna Rae observing to Roma that the more you knew about some people, the better you liked dogs. Just then he saw something. A light. Yes. There it was again. Without turning from the window, he motioned with his hand. "Turn off the lights! The lights! Turn 'em off!"

Buddy got the lamp closest to the door. Roma flipped the wall switch. "Don't turn on that flashlight, either," he said to Buddy.

"What was it?" Roma whispered.

What did he see? Edna Rae wanted to know.

Down on the road, Jennings said. Headlights. It looked to him like the car had pulled over. The lights had gone off. But then there was another light. He might have known!—Known what?—That Cecil wasn't finished with him yet. Of course, he knew that Cecil Pedigo had been accused of burning down people's barns. Surely Edna Rae knew that was a part of the Pedigo heritage, burning barns. A Pedigo's God-given right!— What was he going to do? Why, he'd have to go down there, and see if it really was Cecil. Yes, he had to go. He was hurt, yes, but if he didn't go—he was moving around the dark room now, feeling his way to a cabinet drawer; he found the pistol and stuck it behind his belt—if he didn't go, he'd probably be hurt worse: he'd be out a barn.—If he went down there, then Roma was going with him.—No, she'd stay right where she was. With Edna Rae and Buddy. He'd be right back. There it was again. A light. Did they see that? There.

Where? Roma hadn't seen it.

Nor had Edna Rae.

Buddy did. Buddy saw it.

25

While Roma and Edna Rae and Buddy peered out the window, Jennings picked up his six-cell flashlight and slipped out of the house. The first lights he'd seen—after the discovery of the jackrocks in the tires he'd thought immediately of Cecil, and it had occurred to him that Cecil might have launched a whole campaign of retaliations—the first lights he'd seen while staring out the window had been car lights. On the road, straight across the branch from the big barn. Then, later, there was another light. Had to have been a flashlight. He couldn't be sure, but it appeared to be on the branch bank. Just for a second or two. If it was Cecil—and it had to be—Cecil had probably needed light to come up through the willows on the branch bank below the barn.

Jennings needed no light. At least not yet. If there was any spot of earth he knew, by day or by night, it was this place. The big barn loomed black against the sky a hundred yards ahead of him. Here was the fence, the cattle gap. He took the pistol—

his Dad's old .38—out of his belt, bent down, slipped through the bars, and then put the pistol back in his belt.

Would Cecil have a gun? He hadn't appeared to have one at The Trading Post this afternoon. Just the blackjack. And he didn't have that now. Still, there was no way of knowing, and gun or no gun, the thing to do, if it was Cecil, was to get the drop on him. Be in place before Cecil knew anyone was around.

He moved silently toward the upper side of the black barn. When he reached the barn, he leaned against it, on the back side, where it was darkest, and listened. Thought he heard something—something clicking. With his back to the upper side of the barn, he moved toward the far end, the flashlight in his left, the pistol in his right hand. At the far end of the barn, at the very corner, by the old corn wagon that had stood there for years, he stopped again. Listened. Yes, something stirring. This put him in mind of stalking squirrels, years ago. He'd be just under the crest of a ridge and over on the other side, halfway down, maybe, he could hear a stirring in the leaves. Or, standing under a tall hickory tree, he couldn't see the squirrel, high up, but he could hear the squirrel cutting a hickory nut, and see the cuttings sifting down through the leaves.

Now it was the width of the barn between him and Cecil, who would have got out of his car, come across the little bottom to the branch, crossed the branch, and climbed the steep branch bank, through willows, to the barn. That would have been where Cecil turned on his light for a few seconds, when he had to come up through the willows. All Jennings had to do now was cross to the side of the barn nearest the branch and the road, look around the corner of the barn, and he would know. Know whether he had imagined this whole thing, or whether Cecil—or someone—was there.

He crossed to the branch bank side of the barn. The ground

was soft and damp here. Always had been. Wet weather spring, his father had said. And in rainy periods, Jennings had seen water ooze from the bank at that end of the barn. His back against the barn, flashlight in his left, pistol in his right hand still, he looked around the corner of the barn.

What he saw he first took to be a stump—a dark stumplike mass, no more than two or three feet high, halfway down the barn's length, about where the feed room and harness racks were. Or it could have been a large dog, totally engrossed in the carcass of something it had killed, or come on. The dark mass shifted. No stump. Then it stood. No dog.

Jennings turned the corner of the barn, crouched, and turned his light on the standing figure. He trained the light full in the figure's face.

Yeah, Cecil. Cecil's face, under his Cordell County Deputy Sheriff hat, with the usual reddish stubble. A furtive, ground-hog face. He turned his head away to avoid the light.

"Cecil, goddam you," Jennings said, "get your hands up against the side of the barn!" He pulled back the hammer on the revolver, gave it a good *snick-click* that Cecil could hear.

Cecil moved. He turned slowly, took two deliberate steps to the side of the barn, and placed his hands against it.

"Higher! Up over your head!" Jennings said.

Cecil reached higher. In the bright beam of Jennings' light, Cecil's hands were the rusty color of watersnakes.

"Now, if you don't want to get shot, you keep them right there, Cecil," Jennings said.

"You don't have to shoot," Cecil said, craning around toward Jennings.

"Keep your face to the barn!" Jennings said. "I don't want to have to look at your sorry face! Mess with me, I'll shoot you without having to. Just for the fun of it.—Now you stand still, and I mean still."—He poked Cecil's hip pockets with the barrel of the .38, feeling for any pistol Cecil might be carrying. He felt around for anything in Cecil's front pockets. Maybe he carried his pistol in his belt, the way Jennings had shoved the old revolver into his own belt.

This was awkward. There was only one way to search Cecil. "OK, Cecil, step back."

Cecil stepped back from the barn and as Jennings followed Cecil with his light, he glimpsed the gasoline can. And beside it on the ground, Cecil's flashlight. Jennings swung his own light back and forth between the round, red one-gallon container with a spout, and Cecil.

The sight of the can enraged Jennings, and looking at it, sitting there on the ground, he remembered the time when Cecil and a couple of the Barnes boys had stolen Jennings' clothes off a bush by the creek, while Jennings was in swimming, and thrown his shoes in the creek (they'd washed away). "You sorry sonofabitch!" Jennings crossed and stood by the gas can. "Take your pants off, Cecil." Jennings moved his light up and down Cecil's length. Cecil stood there, looking as if he didn't believe Jennings. Jennings swung the bright light back and forth across Cecil's face, blinding him. "Take off your pants! Move!"

Cecil turned, as if from shyness, and started to loosen his belt.

"No, goddam you, keep your hands where I can see them!" Jennings said.

Cecil appeared confused. He raised his hands over his head again and stood with his back to Jennings. "How am I gonna. . . . ?"

"Turn around to me here, so I can see your hands!"

Cecil obliged.

"Now drop your pants."

Cecil did.

"Step out of them."

Cecil stood on one leg and danced around a little as he came out of his pants.

Cecil wore no shorts. And while his forearms and hands were a rusty brown, his legs were grub-white.

"I want your shirt, too, Cecil. Shuck it!"

Standing naked except for shoes and socks, Cecil looked like something you found when you rolled over a rotten log.

Jennings picked up Cecil's pants and started pulling the pockets inside out. He meant to let Cecil have his car keys. But he found no key. Cecil must have left the key in his car over on the road. What he found was some change, a pocketknife, some split shot sinkers, a tin of aspirin. A would-be barn burner who got headaches! He felt a twinge of pain in the back of his head, where Cecil had hit him with the blackjack. "Did Hilliard send you up here to do this?"

Cecil shook his head back and forth violently. No.

Jennings knew Cecil would tell a lie as naturally as he breathed, but Cecil's quick and emphatic denial seemed genuine. "This your own doing, then. That right?"

Cecil looked down at the ground. "That's right."

"Hilliard sent you to try and run me off the road, though, didn't he?"

Again Cecil shook his head no.

"You lying to me, Cecil?"

No.

"Trying to run me off the road, picking a fight at The Trading Post, that was all your doing, too?"

Yeah, it was all his idea.

"I figured Hilliard wouldn't be dumb enough to send you up here after that school board meeting," Jennings said. "But I thought maybe Hilliard. . . ." There was no point in going on. Jennings figured he'd never know the truth of it.

He shook the contents of Cecil's pockets onto the ground beside Cecil's flashlight. "I want to tell you something, Cecil. You better hope lightning don't strike this barn and burn it down. Because if it burns, I'm coming for you. You better hope bad wiring in my house don't start a fire and burn the house down. Because if it does, I'm coming for you. If anything burns, Cecil, I'm coming for you. And I'll kill you, Cecil. And if you don't get your sorry ass gone, right now, I may just kill you now!"

Cecil wanted his pants.

Hell, no! Cecil wasn't getting his pants.

At least, then, let him have his shirt.

Cecil wasn't getting his shirt, either. If Cecil didn't start walking. . . .

Cecil got his flashlight and walked. Jennings held Cecil's white buttocks in the beam of light as he disappeared down the branch bank, then reappeared climbing the other side. He stood there until he heard Cecil's car start up over on the road. He saw the headlights come on, saw the car turn in the road and pull away.

Jennings eased the hammer down on the .38 and shoved it down between his belt and shirt. He gathered up Cecil's pants and shirt, draped them over his left arm, and, picking up the gas can, started back toward the house.

He got a twitch under his left eye, and he muttered to himself as rage surged through him. He would. By God, he'd kill Cecil Pedigo. If anything burned. He just halfway hoped something did . . . so he could kill the sorry sonofabitch.

26

Reentering the house proved to be more dangerous than confronting Cecil, for when he came up onto the porch in the dark Roma and Edna Rae and Buddy feared he might be Cecil, or whoever it was down there at the barn. He should have known they'd be afraid and would try to protect themselves, but he was surprised, when he pushed open the door and turned on his flashlight, to discover Edna Rae crouched with a poker, holding it like a baseball bat, and Roma and Buddy brandishing butcher knives.

"It's just me," he said. "Good Lord!"

Was it him, was it Cecil? Buddy wanted to know.

Yeah. Did they see the car turn, over on the road?

They saw it. Looked like it headed back towards Jewell Hill.

Jennings guessed it was all right to turn on a light now, and when Buddy flipped the switch there Jennings stood, the pistol in his belt, Cecil's clothes and the gas can in his left hand, his flashlight in the other.

What was all that? Roma wanted to know.

Jennings held up the can.

Gasoline, Edna Rae said.

Jennings sniffed the can, then held it out for them to smell. It appeared to be No. 1 kerosene, but just as good to burn a barn.

Was Cecil going to use those rags to start the fire? Roma asked.

Rags? These are Cecil's clothes, his pants and shirt!

You made him strip? Buddy asked gleefully.

Well, what did Jennings want with the carcass? The hide was enough.

Jennings set down the gas can. He picked up a stapler off his worktable, and, motioning for Buddy to help him, stapled the shirt and pants to the wall, so they were displayed like the skin of an animal. They'd heard of nailing somebody's hide to the wall, hadn't they?

They all began to chatter at once. Roma, hand to her mouth at the prospect of Cecil driving toward Jewell Hill with no pants or shirt. What would Cecil do? Edna Rae wondered. Get some clothes, Jennings figured. What about his beeper? Buddy wondered. Cecil wasn't wearing his beeper; must've left that in the car. Buddy howled at the thought of Cecil heading out in his old Pontiac wearing nothing but his shoes, shorts, and beeper. Just his shoes and his beeper, Jennings guessed, because Cecil hadn't been wearing any shorts.

Jennings wanted a Running Jack. So did Roma. As he mixed the drinks, Roma wanted to know if there was going to be a feud now. Would Jennings have to sit up every night, watching for Cecil, wondering if he would try to burn the barn again, or the house? Jennings didn't think so. Anyway, the problem wasn't so much Cecil as it was Hilliard. Cecil just did what he was told to do. Mostly. But if Jennings had to, yes, he'd sit up

208

nights. He'd fight. Fight Hilliard *and* Cecil. He wasn't going to be burnt out, run off.

Edna Rae said if it came to it, they'd all help. Take turns sitting up, watching—she and Roma and Buddy. Buddy detailed an elaborate trap he could make—a big hole covered with sticks and leaves, that would have big sharp sticks in the bottom of it, so if Cecil came around the barn again, he'd fall in it. Jennings wasn't taken with the idea. Nor with Buddy's wanting to get started right then on fixing the flats on Jennings' car. No, they would do that tomorrow. Now they needed to get Edna Rae on home. And they did, all riding in Roma's Mercury.

Now we're gonna get shed of you, Jennings told Buddy. And he directed Roma, who was driving, to take Buddy to her house so he could get to bed. It was already past midnight.

What're you all gonna do? Buddy wanted to know.

Ride over to the mall in Jewell Hill and see that whale, Jennings teased. He winked at Roma.

Buddy knew that was a lie. They wouldn't have that whale at the mall this late at night. He still wanted to see that whale, though.

Get on in the house and get to bed, Jennings said. Slowly, Buddy turned away from the car and headed for the door.

Jennings jerked his head toward Buddy. Like trying to push a chain, he said to Roma. And he leaned over and kissed her.

27

"What do you think?" he asked Roma.

Roma waited until she saw Buddy turn on a light in the house. Then she leaned over and kissed him back. That's what she thought.

She'd been driving and was behind the wheel of the Mercury. Jennings got out, walked around, and scooted her to the passenger side.

"Are you sure you want to drive?" Roma asked. "You must be hurting still, and absolutely exhausted. It's after midnight, Jennings."

"I feel fine, Roma," he said. He felt better than fine. It made no sense, he knew, but he was surging with energy and strength. He started the car, turned, and rolled down the drive. As he pulled out onto the highway he pushed in a tape—of a blind street singer from southwest Virginia doing "Time Has Made a Change."—"Back in days gone by,"—the voice creaked like old saddle leather—"when I was young and strong/ I could climb the hillsides all day long."

He was home, he told Roma. Home to stay. He had so many things to tell her. He'd left because he'd felt he couldn't stay, felt he didn't belong here any longer. Then he'd found out he couldn't stay away. And after this day—this strange day—and the fight with Cecil, the school meeting, the second run-in with Cecil—after all that, Newfound was starting to feel like it used to feel, before he ever left.

How was that? Roma asked.

Mean, and sweet. Newfound and Cordell County was Cecil, and Hilliard, and that was mean. But it was Roma, too, and she was sweet.

Roma allowed she wasn't sugar, nor salt, nor anybody's honey.

Yes, she was.

She wondered if Jennings realized what he'd said to Buddy this evening. He'd said: "I'm not your daddy, son."

He'd said that?

Yes. But he still could be a father to Buddy. He already acted like he was.

Well, Roma shouldn't forget who'd been acting like a mama to him since he got sick.—Jennings was silent a long time, listening to the tape, driving, thinking, remembering. He remembered now—why now?—a cartoon showing a bunch of Vikings setting out in their ship, while on the shore a group of stout Viking women waved goodbye with one arm and held a squalling brat in the other. Children wrestled on the ground at the feet of the women, beat each other on their little horned helmets, and created general disorder. One of the Viking women asked another: "What is it, I wonder, that makes them set out toward God knows where?"

211

Jennings chuckled and remembered standing several years ago in his backyard on a warm evening in early October when the air was soft and the darkness felt like mole fur, like a horse's velvety nose. An evening like this one. He and his wife had argued, and as always, her daughter created a diversion to make them stop. That time she'd asked him to come outside and look at the moon with her. Still seething, he'd gone out and stood looking up while his step-daughter—she'd been about thirteen then—showed him the woman in the moon. She said the woman in the moon was sitting in front of a mirror with her back to them, putting on lipstick and eye shadow. Rattling on nervously, she'd reminded him that it was he who'd first taught her to see not only the man in the moon but, looking at it another way, the woman in the moon, too.—Now Jennings was remembering that evening, the girl's nervous smile, itself a thin quarter moon, and thinking about the Vikings cartoon.— "What is it, I wonder, that makes them set out toward God knows where?"—when he came to the Newfound Church sign. He turned off, drove past the church, and on up the hill toward the cemetery.

"Time has made a change in the old homeplace," the blind street singer mourned. "Time has made a change in each smiling face."

There was a turn-around on top of the hill, he remembered. He'd driven up here one night about a month ago. You circled two hickory trees, he remembered. As well by night as by day. He whipped through the curves, climbing the hill. "And I know my friends can plainly see/Time has made a change in me." The street singer went into the next stanza as Jennings pulled around the trees, stopped, and turned the key back so the tape kept playing.

He reached for the makings, in the back seat, and mixed

two Runnings Jacks. They sat drinking, listening. Roma put on another tape—one with a Tom T. Hall song that began, "I guess I should have written, Dad, to let you know that I was coming home." Jennings smiled in the dark. Roma knew what she was doing, his father's grave right out there on the hill. His mother's, too. And her brother Craig's grave. Wasn't it?

Yes.

After Craig's death, he asked, had Roma felt about Newfound and Cordell County—about home—the way Jennings felt after his father's death? In that dogwood winter of grief, after his father died, he'd turned away from the grave, as if— into another country. His father's life, subtracted from this place, altered fields and hills. He'd seemed a sudden stranger to himself here. He'd been home—but not home. He'd turned away, his heart fluttering like a sparrow beating its wings at a window inside a house standing solitary and empty in a field. It was as if, beyond a baffling hard transparency, there were cedars, fenced fields, light, air, country he came from. He could see it but couldn't go there again. If he could only go there!

"Right by your Mama and Daddy's graves?" Roma asked.

"It won't bother my Daddy," Jennings said. He worked her skirt up over her thighs until it circled her waist. "I've already loved you—in my mind," he told her.

"And now you're gonna love me out of your mind. Is that it?"

"No. I'm gonna love you out of your mind."

"What did you think it would be like?"

"Like this."

He'd wondered, now he knew. She was countryside he knew at night, turns he knew how to lean into. A roadside grown up in goldenrods, staghorn sumac standing looking down like deer. Field of Queen Anne's Lace. Found me in a field. Found her in a field. Far end of a field. A house. Slow, steady. Rain on the roof. An untended orchard where branches drooped, heavy with apples that fell into waist-high orchard grass. Woods. Water. Amber turn signals . . . like fireflies . . . the yellow line in the road up the Sugar Creek Road . . . the Shell sign at The Trading Post, or that patch of goldenrod between the pond and the barns. He was going far back—where love and death and beauty all felt the same. O Beautiful Star. Roma. She rose and fell like a long wave and he felt headed into some fabulous adventure . . . that night years ago on a student ship headed for Europe, the ship moved out of the harbor and for the first time he felt the swell of the ocean, the ship rose . . . and rose, and then fell, it seemed, forever. The ship. Roma. She moaned. Setting out, toward God knows where, toward something shining white, far away on a hill. He had been there once. He was going there again—coming home, to his first, best country, now strange and new.

28

Dear Gerald,

I'm sure you won't remember, but the night before you left Newfound years ago, we were together back on the Bearwallow, and I promised to write to you.

Well, I'm writing, finally. I got your address from Edna Rae.

I'm back in Newfound and intend to stay. Bought the old Shelton house, dismantled it, and now that we've come through the winter, I'm putting it back together here at the homeplace. With help.

Surely you remember Roseanne Shelton. She brought her boy back here some years ago and he's grown up here. He's helping. I've sort of adopted him.

And you remember the Livesays, but maybe not one of the younger girls, Roma. We got to know one another when I came back and we're what you'd call an item now.

Roma and Roseanne's boy and I amount to a kind of mix-and-stir family.

I'm picking a little guitar and waiting for the redhorse to run!
Come see us. Stay a spell!

Your cousin,
Robert Jennings Wells

This book has been set in Fairfield Medium
designed by Rudolph Ruzicka. Composition by Tseng
Information Systems, Inc. Printing and
binding by Thomson-Shore, Inc.